THE
Twenty-Four-Hour
LIPSTICK MYSTERY

THE
Twenty-Four-Hour
LIPSTICK MYSTERY
BONNIE PRYOR

ILLUSTRATED BY
SHEILA HAMANAKA

MORROW JUNIOR BOOKS / NEW YORK

Library of Congress Cataloging-in-Publication Data
Pryor, Bonnie.
The twenty-four-hour lipstick mystery / Bonnie Pryor :
illustrations by Sheila Hamanaka.
p. cm.
Summary: To earn money for charm school, eleven-year-old
Cassie works for the owner of a spooky mansion and
uncovers a mystery surrounding a secret room.
ISBN 0-688-08198-3
[1. Mystery and detective stories. 2. Mansions—Fiction.]
I. Hamanaka, Sheila, ill. II. Title.
PZ7.P94965Tw 1989
[Fic]—dc20 89-34483 CIP AC

To **CHRISSY,**
a princess who loves a good mystery

CONTENTS

——— ONE ———

Mrs. DuPrey's School of Beauty and Charm

My bratty brother Daniel slammed the front door, threw his books on the hall table, and headed straight for the kitchen.

"You are supposed to ask me before you get into stuff," I yelled as he opened the refrigerator door. "That's for dessert."

He ignored me and helped himself to a heaping bowl of ice cream. "There is someone moving into the old Murdock place," he announced importantly.

"You're crazy. Who would want to live in that creepy place?"

"I am not crazy. I saw a moving van in the driveway and some men were carrying in furniture."

I was torn between fuming at Danny and curiosity about his news. I could not imagine anyone in their right mind moving into the decaying old mansion, which is around the corner and down two blocks from where we live. The grounds take up a whole block, and most of them are covered with thick woods that almost encircle the house. The mansion stands back from the road, a relic of long ago surrounded by modern split-levels and ranch-style houses, like ours. Everyone says the Murdock house is more than a hundred years old, and parts of it look ready to cave in any minute. Most of the people in the neighborhood would love to see it torn down. It was bad enough when old Mr. Murdock lived there. He was so crabby no one liked to go near the house. But at least he was rich enough to have a gardener keep up the grounds. It's been empty since he died nearly six months ago, and day by day it gets older and creepier. A lot of the younger kids think it's haunted. Lately there have been stories about strange lights floating around at night. People say it's the ghost of Mr. Murdock. Of course I don't believe in ghosts, but I have to admit I'm not crazy about walking past the house at night.

I gave Danny a suspicious look. "Is this another one of your jokes?"

"Go look for yourself if you don't believe me."

"I can't, creep. I have to stay home and baby-sit you. Remember?"

"How could I forget? You've griped about it every afternoon since Mom went to work."

"It isn't fair. You go off to Arnold's house every day, and I sit here by myself," I said.

"It isn't my fault Mom got a job," Danny said.

I shrugged, my mind still on the Murdock house.

"I wonder who would want to live in a house like that?" I said, thinking out loud.

"Probably another witch like you," Danny taunted. He stuck out his tongue for emphasis. Danny is ten and his main purpose in life is to drive me crazy. You might say that his life is a marvelous success.

"I wish I was a witch," I said. "My first project would be to turn you into a frog."

"Too late. You already worked that spell on yourself," Danny jeered as he opened the front door. "I'm going to Arnold's to play football," he yelled, and dashed down the street.

I put the ice cream away and slumped down in a chair in front of the TV, jabbing at the remote control. There was still an hour to kill before Mom got home. Usually I used this time to practice my piano lesson and start on homework, but after Danny's taunt I was too glum.

The problem is that I really do look like a frog. My eyes are too big and my mouth too wide. On top of that, my nose is crooked. Mom says I just need to grow into my face, whatever that means. She says I will be pretty someday. But of course mothers are supposed to say things like that. And even if it was true, it doesn't help me now.

I flipped around the stations before giving up in disgust. There was nothing on except for soap operas, which I figure only someone with a moron's intelligence could enjoy, and cartoons, which are even worse. I got my books and sat down at the

dining-room table. I considered walking to the Murdock house to check out Danny's story. But Mom sometimes called before she left work at the furniture store, and she would worry if no one answered the phone. I was supposed to watch "things" until she got home. The main "thing" I had to watch was Danny, even though I was only one year older.

The paper boy threw the paper on the porch hard enough to knock the house off its foundation. I yanked open the door to really tell him off, but he was already three doors up the street. I noticed with satisfaction that Mr. Wilson had come out of his front door and was yelling and shaking his finger. I couldn't hear what he said, but the boy was standing with his head down, looking embarrassed. Serves you right, I thought. I brought the paper in and put it on the hall table.

Danny's books were already there. I scooped them up and headed for his room. There was no sense putting Mom in a bad mood when she came home. Our messiness had never bothered her before she went back to work, but now she was always tired in the evening.

I threw Danny's books on his bed and picked up his latest puzzle book, which was on his nightstand. Danny loves to work crossword puzzles and cryptograms. There was something else on his nightstand. When I picked it up I saw it was a tiny deer carved out of wood. I turned it over in my hands, marveling. Danny's dresser tops and shelves are filled with miniature castles and sky-scrapers he made out of toy bricks. I have to admit they are pretty clever. But this was different. The deer's head was slightly tilted as though it sensed some nearby danger. It looked so real I could almost imagine it darting away the minute I set it down.

I suddenly remembered the social studies quiz I was supposed to cut out of the paper. Every week it was printed on the back of the sports page. I didn't dare cut it out before Dad read the paper, and when I waited until after dinner more often than not I forgot it. That didn't make my teacher, Mrs. Simkins, very happy. I went back to the hall and glanced at the headlines as I unfolded the paper. Someone had stolen some old, valuable jewelry while the owner was at a party. There had been a string of burglaries lately, and the police couldn't seem to catch the thieves. Lexington is usually a pretty quiet town. It's the kind of place where people don't worry too much about locking their doors. But now the police were warning people to lock their valuables in a safe. I chuckled as I flipped the page. Even if we had a safe we wouldn't have much to put in it.

I found the quiz and checked the back of the page. I was in luck. There was only an advertisement on the back. I checked it carefully to make sure it wasn't important.

"Mrs. DuPrey's School of Beauty and Charm," the ad said in big letters. Mrs. DuPrey guaranteed to give all young ladies between the ages of ten and fifteen the poise and confidence of a model in ten short weeks.

Poise. I liked the sound of that word. Even if a person was destined to look like a frog all her life, she might be all right if she had poise and confidence.

There was only one catch. The lessons cost $79.95, and they started in a month. The ad went on to say that the $79.95 was a special introductory price. The usual rate was $100.

I had a feeling it didn't matter if it was a reduced price. Mom and Dad would probably say they couldn't afford it. I thought about offering to give up piano lessons, but decided against it. Mom had her heart set on my becoming a famous pianist.

Dumping my piggy bank on my bed, I counted out my entire life savings. One dollar and eighty-seven cents. I counted again to make sure I hadn't made a mistake. Actually, it turned out that I had. There was only one dollar and eighty-six cents. I wished I'd seen Mrs. DuPrey's advertisement before I'd blown most of my savings, plus two weeks allowance in advance, on a sweater I'd seen at Olson's Department Store.

Sara had been my best friend since the first grade. I decided I would call her. Maybe she would have some ideas about how I could get the rest of the money.

"Did you see the ad for Mrs. DuPrey's School of

Beauty and Charm?" I asked her. When she said she hadn't I explained, but I had the feeling she was only half listening.

"I'm watching 'One Love,' she said, referring to a popular soap opera. "There is this girl named Lana who—"

"I hate those things," I said. "I'm trying to talk to you about real life."

"Well, maybe your parents will pay for the lessons," she said. "What time do they start?"

I consulted the ad. "Right after school."

"Mom would probably pay for me to go. But I'd miss 'One Love.' "

From then on, her side of the conversation was mostly uh-huhs and mmmms as she continued to watch the show. After a few minutes I gave up. Maybe my parents would understand how I felt. Mrs. DuPrey's charm school sounded like the answer to all my problems. But I wasn't very optimistic. If I couldn't convince my best friend how important the lessons were, how could I talk my parents into forking out $79.95?

The conversation at dinner went pretty much like I expected.

"I'm sorry, Cassie. We can't afford it right now," Mom said.

"Maybe you could earn the money," Dad suggested.

"The lessons start next month," I said. "How could I earn that much money in one month? No

8

one would hire an eleven-year-old. And anyway, I'm always stuck here baby-sitting Danny."

"That is just too much money," Mom said. "And as for baby-sitting, one hour a day is hardly 'always stuck.' "

"Maybe you could use your allowance more wisely and go another time," Dad said sympathetically.

"I know how you could earn some money," Danny piped in. "You could hire yourself out to parties as the birthday frog."

"That's enough, Danny," said Dad.

"Your sister is a very pretty girl," Mom said. I kicked Danny under the table.

"Ribbit," he muttered.

"What did you say?" Dad asked.

"Oh, excuse me," Danny said, the picture of innocence. "I burped."

I kicked him again, but he only grinned.

TWO

The Murdock House

"Why did you do such a dumb thing?" Sara asked that Saturday morning.

We were sitting on my bed counting my meager finances for the third time.

"I couldn't help it," I said. "The words just popped out of my mouth before I could stop them."

"Well, it was dumb, if you don't mind me telling you," Sara said.

I really did mind her saying it, especially twice, although I had to agree. The day after my conversation with my parents I had overheard Missy Ryan talking about Mrs. DuPrey's charm school in the girls' rest room at school. Missy Ryan needs charm school like I need a hole in my head. She is already the prettiest girl in class, with big blue eyes and hair down to her waist. All the boys in the room are madly in love with her, even the ones who hate girls. If she got any more charming I might as well move to the desert and become a hermit.

"I was thinking about going, too," I blurted out.

Now this is what I mean about Missy. You can't even hate her. She smiled at me and grabbed my hands. "Oh, that's wonderful. It will be so much more fun going with someone I know."

Dawn Reynolds was sitting on the edge of a sink. "Your parents would never throw their money away on something as dumb as charm school," she sneered. "Although in your case it might be a good investment." Dawn has never forgiven me for winning both the spelling bee and the art contest in third grade. She was second in both.

"My parents already told me I could." The words popped out before I could stop them.

So here I was, still with only one dollar and eighty-six cents, wondering how I could earn the rest.

"I think I have seven pennies," said Sara, adding them to the pile.

"Thanks a lot."

"If you don't want them . . ."

"No," I said quickly. "I want them. But where am I going to get seventy-eight more dollars? Haven't you got a couple of dollars you could lend me?"

Sara hesitated. "I do have a little bit saved," she said. "But I wanted to buy that skirt that goes with your sweater. When I do, can I borrow your sweater to wear with it?"

I nodded reluctantly. Sara had talked me into buying the sweater in the first place. An ugly thought ran through my mind. Had she planned on borrowing it all the time? I wasn't so sure it looked all that great on me, although in the store Sara had insisted it did.

There was an awkward silence. "Too bad you're not old enough to get baby-sitting jobs. Except for little brothers, that is," she added with a chuckle. "Tell your folks you want to be paid for watching Danny."

"They gave me a raise in my allowance," I said. "But I spent it on a sweater, remember?"

"Maybe you could find some odd jobs," Sara said.

"Oh, sure. That's what my dad suggested. But most people give you a dollar for a job. That means I only have to find seventy-eight jobs."

We sat thinking for a few minutes. "Mom gives me twenty-five cents a day for milk. If I saved that I'd have one dollar and twenty-five cents a week," I said finally. "That's five dollars in a month." It wasn't much, but it was all I could think of. I waited for Sara to at least offer her milk money, but she didn't.

"What are you girls doing in here on such a nice day?" Dad said, passing my room and poking his head in the door. "You should be outside getting some fresh air."

Dad is a nut about fresh air. It was nice out, but

he would have said the same thing if it was twenty below.

"We were just going," I called out, scraping the pennies into the piggy bank. Then I whispered to Sara, "Let's get out of here before he thinks of some work for me to do, like raking leaves or something."

"Maybe he would pay you."

I shook my head. "Dad thinks that everyone should pitch in without being paid. He says that is just being part of the family."

"I'm glad my mother's not like that. She gives me a quarter every time I set the table."

"My dad says he is building our character. Right now I would rather build my bank account."

"Where should we go?" Sara asked, pulling on her sweater.

"Let's walk by the Murdock house," I suggested. "Maybe we could get a peek at the people who moved in."

We walked up the street in the warm autumn sunshine. The leaves were already red and gold, and enough of them had fallen to make a pleasant crackling, swishing sound under our feet. I was glad Dad had chased us outside, because even the air smelled fresh and sweet. It was a day that made you glad to be alive, even if you did have desperate money problems.

Sara and I chatted about school, but as we turned the corner onto Elm Street we both fell silent. The good feeling seemed to disappear as we reached the edge of the Murdock property. Here the trees were taller—thick, heavy evergreens that blocked the view of the house. The woods at the edge of the property were so choked with undergrowth that they seemed gloomy and mysterious even in the bright sun. An involuntary shudder went up my spine. There was definitely something spooky about the Murdock house. I knew Sara was feeling the same way. Usually the only time she is not yakking is when she is watching "One Love." But now she was quiet and her face was pale and solemn.

The house actually faced Fifth Street, but the drive that curled lazily to the front of the house opened onto Elm. As we passed the driveway I slowed down for a better look at the house. It was huge. The front of the house was mostly stone and crumbling brick. There were three stories in the main part, and a huge stone tower separated that section from a newer-looking wing. A straight row of narrow windows marched across the first floor on the side that faced Elm Street, interrupted in the middle by a high octagonal window. It made me think of a cyclops with one strange eye in the middle. The only thing normal-looking was the two workmen on the roof doing repairs.

"This would make a great setting for a horror movie," I said, trying to joke.

Sara laughed nervously; then she motioned for me to be quiet. There was a man clearing some brush in front of the house, and a boy I remembered

14

from school was trimming hedges by the entrance.

"That's the new boy in Mr. Muldorn's homeroom at school," Sara whispered. "He just moved to Lexington a few weeks ago. I think he's cute, don't you?"

I shrugged, pretending I hadn't noticed him before. Actually, I had spotted him the first day even though he was in the seventh grade, a year ahead of us.

"I think his name is Jason," Sara said, just as he looked up from his work and waved.

I groaned. "He's seen us. Let's get out of here."

"Why?" Sara asked innocently. She waved back.

"Did you want to see Miss Murdock?" Jason called.

"No, actually we were just—" Sara didn't let me finish. She gave Jason a bright smile.

"Cassie wants to talk to her about a job," Sara said smoothly. "She wants to earn some money so she can—" It was my turn to interrupt before Sara told him my whole life story.

"Is she home?" I asked. My mind was whirling desperately. I glared at Sara for getting me into this mess, but she pretended not to notice.

"She's home," said Jason. "I don't know if she needs any help, but it might be worth a try. She hired me." He gestured to the man who was raking leaves into a huge pile. "She thought Mr. Bemiss might need some help getting this yard back in shape."

"A lot of people think this house is haunted," I said as Jason opened the gate.

"Do you?"

"Of course not. But you have to admit that it's kind of creepy."

"Oh, I don't know. I kind of like it. Of course it needs a lot of fixing up."

"What is Miss Murdock like?" I asked.

The gardener, Mr. Bemiss, looked up and gave us a long hard stare. Jason mumbled something about getting back to work, leaving me to face the long walk to the door by myself. I turned and looked helplessly at Sara. She had gotten me into this predicament, and now she was leaning comfortably on the gate, waving me on.

Miss Murdock is probably a little old lady, I told myself. She probably has white hair and a shawl and maybe she even walks with a cane. By the time I had reached the big front door I had almost convinced myself. A little old lady like that might really need help. It would be kind of like a good deed, even if I did get paid for it.

As I reached for the knocker—some kind of hideous gargoyle, naturally—I was aware that the eyes of the dour gardener had followed me all the way up the drive. The door was about ten feet high and it looked like it ought to be opened by a butler named Igor. I glanced back at Sara once more just as the door swung slowly open.

"I was just washing my hair," apologized the

17

young woman who stood in the doorway, a towel wrapped around her head like a turban. "Can I help you?"

The woman was young and seemed vaguely familiar. She was absolutely gorgeous, even dressed in blue jeans and a sweat shirt. She had long dark lashes that framed beautiful green eyes, and I saw wisps of pale blonde hair escaping the towel. Her nails were long and perfectly manicured. Not exactly the helpless little old lady I'd pictured.

I suddenly remembered I had to breathe when I exploded in a fit of coughing. "I'm Cassie Adams. I was wondering if you needed any work. I mean if I needed any work. I mean I . . ." I couldn't seem to get the words out straight. I coughed and choked again.

"Let me get you some water," the woman said. She took me by the arm and led me to a chair completely surrounded by boxes. She motioned for me to sit and disappeared down the hall. I huddled miserably in the chair until she returned, aware that I had sounded like a total idiot.

I glanced around the room while I waited. The outside light barely cut through the grimy windows, and there were cobwebs hanging from the ceiling. It was not a cheerful place to sit by myself. I was relieved to hear the click of high heels as the woman returned.

"Now," she said, handing me the water, "let's start over. Do I understand you are looking for a job?"

I blurted out the whole story, telling her about Mrs. DuPrey's charm school and my empty piggy bank. "So that's why I need a job, Miss Murdock," I finished.

The woman smiled. "Oh, I'm not Miss Murdock. My name is Victoria Presser. I'm Miss Murdock's secretary. Miss Murdock is—"

"Right here," said a second voice. "I was in the next room and I heard. How are you, Cassie?" Miss Murdock shook my hand firmly and smiled. She was plain-looking, a little older than Victoria Presser. Severe wire-rimmed glasses slipped down her nose, and she pushed them back up with an irritated motion. She sat down on a pile of boxes and studied me for a minute. "As you can see, we do need some help," she said, waving to the cluttered room. "But you seem a little young."

"I'll work hard," I promised.

She still looked doubtful, but Victoria Presser spoke up. "She could unpack and shelve the books. She has a very important reason for needing a job." She gave me a conspiratorial wink.

"All right. Maybe we can help each other," Miss Murdock said, relenting. "How does two dollars an hour sound?" When I nodded eagerly, she continued. "If your parents agree, you can come for a couple of hours each day after school and maybe on Saturdays. As a matter of fact, you could start Monday. Everything is such a mess. The movers just dumped the boxes, and Vicky worries about breaking her fingernails." I thought I heard a faint edge of scorn in her voice, but I could understand Victoria Presser's concern. My own nails were always short and ragged. If I could grow nails like hers I wouldn't take a chance on breaking them, either.

"I could help you right now." I jumped up eagerly and reached for the nearest crate. "No, no, not that one," Miss Murdock said quickly. "I'll take care of that one. It is much too heavy." It was a wooden crate nailed shut and stamped "Fragile. Breakable."

I jerked my hand away. Maybe it was filled with priceless antiques. Miss Murdock must be very rich to own a house like this, even though it was run-down.

"I'll get back to my hair," Victoria Presser said. As she left the room a little frown passed over Miss Murdock's face and I wondered if she was jealous of her beautiful secretary. "I'm in the middle of a job right now," Miss Murdock called after her pleasantly enough. "Why don't you explain to Cassie what we are doing? I think I'll have her work on the books." She gave me a brisk handshake. "I will see you on Monday." Then she pushed the crate to a corner, out of the way.

"Come on," Victoria Presser said. "I'll show you the library."

When I left the house a half an hour later, Sara was already gone. Jason looked up from his raking and smiled. "Any luck?"

I nodded. "I'm going to help her sort some books."

"That's great," he said. "I'll see you on Monday then."

I felt myself blushing. He almost sounded like he was glad. But maybe he was just happy to have someone besides Mr. Bemiss to talk with. The sour-faced gardener didn't look like he'd be very good company.

On the way home from the gloomy mansion I thought about Victoria Presser. Maybe someday I could be like her. Not as pretty, perhaps, but I could stand any ordeal to be that smooth and confident. Even though the house still gave me the creeps, it might be fun working there. Miss Murdock had actually been quite nice, although she hadn't talked very much.

As soon as I blurted out my news Mom's nose wrinkled up like it always does when she is upset.

"I wish you had asked first," she said. "We don't know anything about Miss Murdock. And what about Danny? I count on you to watch him after school."

"First you tell me to earn the money, and then you get upset when I do," I wailed. "I am only helping her move in. And Danny is usually over at Arnold's house, anyway."

"It's a good thing she didn't see your room before she hired you," Danny snickered.

I glared at him, but Dad chuckled. "He's got a

point. You do seem to have a hard time keeping your own things in order."

"But this will help me learn how to be organized," I said with a sudden inspiration.

"In that case," Dad said with mock seriousness, "maybe we should pay Miss Murdock." He looked at Mom. "We could see if Arnold's mother would be willing to watch Danny for a few weeks."

"Oh, thank you," I shouted when Mom finally nodded.

"This will just be on a trial basis," Dad said. "And we will want to talk to Miss Murdock first. But I am very proud that you had enough initiative to go out and find a job on your own."

"What does initiative mean?" asked Danny.

"Let me give you an example," said Dad. "When you see that the garbage needs taking out and you do it without being told, that's initiative."

"Is that a hint?" Danny asked in an innocent voice.

"That's an order," Dad said.

"Remember, it's only for a short time, and only if Arnold's mother doesn't mind," Dad said, when Danny had left. "And of course your homework comes first."

"And your piano practice," Mom added.

"I promise," I said happily. "I can do all that after dinner instead of watching television."

"I won't have any complaints about less television," Dad said dryly.

"Why is that woman living in that big house by herself?" Mom asked.

"She's not alone. She has a secretary named Victoria Presser. She told me that Miss Murdock's grandfather left it to her when he died. But it is so run-down no one wants to buy it. So Miss Murdock is fixing it up into an inn. She calls it a 'bed and breakfast.' She thinks she can sell it then. And she's donating a lot of her family's things to the historical society. Victoria Presser is going to catalog everything for her. You ought to see her. She is beautiful."

"Miss Murdock?"

"No, the secretary, Victoria Presser. Isn't Victoria a beautiful name? I think I've seen her someplace. Maybe in the movies. Wouldn't it be wonderful if a real movie star was living in Lexington?"

"Hmm." Mom was hardly listening. "It would be nice if Miss Murdock fixed up the house. It makes me shiver every time I go by. I certainly wouldn't want to live there."

"Why, Alice," teased Dad. "I would almost think you believed in ghosts."

"Well, if I did believe in ghosts, that's the spot I would pick for them to live. I even saw those spooky lights one night coming home from the store."

"You never said anything to me," Dad said.

Mom looked embarrassed. "I wasn't sure what I really saw. It seemed like there was a funny light glowing in the window. I looked away and when I looked back it was gone. Seemed too silly to mention."

"Wow," said Danny, coming back into the room. "That means the Murdock house really is haunted. Wait until I tell everyone my own mother has seen the Murdock ghost."

"Don't you dare tell anyone," Mom said. "There is probably a perfectly logical explanation. The moonlight or something."

All this talk about glowing lights and ghosts was making me nervous. I was almost ready to change my mind. Then I thought of Victoria Presser. Being around such an elegant person, surely some of it would rub off on me. And of course I would get to see Jason every day.

Mom was giving me a strange look. I could almost read her mind. She was wondering if it was safe in that house after all. "Miss Murdock is really nice. You'll see for yourself," I said quickly. "And I'll probably learn a lot of interesting things. Handling all those old books and all," I finished lamely.

The important thing was to earn enough money for Mrs. DuPrey's school. After that I didn't care if I never saw the Murdock house again.

THREE

A Disappearing Cat

Sara was not happy when I told her at school Monday morning that Arnold's mother had agreed to watch Danny and that I could start work that afternoon.

"Why didn't you call and tell me?"

"I didn't know for sure until Mom and Dad talked to Miss Murdock and Arnold's mother," I said. "I'm going to work two hours after school and Saturday afternoons. Miss Murdock said there was enough work for at least a month if I wanted."

"I wouldn't want to work in that house. Is it as creepy inside as it is outside?"

"It's pretty run-down," I admitted.

"I don't know why that dumb old charm school is so important, anyway. If you go to work who's going to go to the movies with me on Saturday?"

I had forgotten. We had been waiting for weeks to see *The Revenge of Damien's Ghost*.

"I'm the one that has to miss it," I said. "And it was your idea to ask for a job in the first place."

"Well, I never thought you would actually get a job," she said. "I was just curious what the inside of the house looked like. You know, if there were any ghosts or anything. Can't you tell Miss Murdock you have a doctor's appointment or something?"

"I don't want to lie to her. And besides, I got the job to earn some money. If I start taking off already I'll never get enough saved."

Sara sniffed. "Keeping your best friend ought to be more important than a stupid job. It won't be any fun alone. I'll have to ask somebody else."

"You didn't want to keep me company at Mrs. DuPrey's charm school," I reminded her. "A dumb soap opera was more important."

"That's different. I've watched 'One Love' for two years," she said, just as the bell rang. She hardly spoke to me the rest of the day.

A little part of me wanted to quit and let everything go back like it was. I could go back to babysitting Danny and listening to my best friend talk about "One Love" or the latest outfit she'd seen at the mall and forget all about Mrs. DuPrey's School of Beauty and Charm. But another part of me was angry. Wasn't a best friend supposed to stick by you, no matter what? I was depressed all day. But when school ended, and I was actually walking to the Murdock house ready for my first day at work, I forgot about Sara. I felt very grown up and mature.

I was so pleased, I waved cheerfully at Danny when I passed him as he was heading to Arnold's house.

When I arrived, Jason smiled and gave me a welcoming wave. "We could walk home together when you're done," he offered. "I go right past your house on the way to mine."

"All right," I agreed happily. I was surprised that he would offer. Then I realized that, being new in town, he probably didn't have many friends. Especially if he had to work every afternoon.

Mr. Bemiss came around the side of the house pushing an empty wheelbarrow. "What are you doing here again?" He frowned.

"I'm going to help Miss Murdock," I answered.

"Well, don't be hanging around out here. Jason's got work to do," he growled.

Just then the door flew open and Victoria Presser, looking glamorous in a red satin blouse and tailored pants, motioned to us. The towel had hidden all but a few wisps of her hair on my last visit, but now I could see it was golden blonde and done in a cascade of curls that surrounded her head like a halo. "I don't suppose you have seen Lucifer, have you?" she asked.

"Lucifer?" I croaked. "The devil?"

Victoria Presser laughed. "Oh, dear. I suppose that did sound peculiar. Lucifer is Miss Murdock's cat. She's daffy about him. He has been gone for hours and Miss Murdock is simply wild with worry. She thinks he might have gotten out."

"I could help you look," I said.

"Would you?" She held open the door. "I think he's in here somewhere taking a nap. It's such a big house, he could be anywhere."

"What does he look like?" I asked.

"He's black and quite large."

"I'll look outside," Jason called as the door swung shut.

Inside, the house was as gloomy and dark as I'd remembered it from my last visit. Thick velvet curtains covered the large windows, and looking up I saw a spiderweb draped across a corner, from the curtain rod to the wall. We started a systematic search of the rooms, looking for the missing Lucifer.

Many of the rooms were empty, or nearly so, and were easily checked. Others were filled with stacks of boxes and some antique furniture. These we searched more thoroughly, peering into each box and behind and under furniture, hoping to see the cat napping in some private spot.

Victoria Presser was getting more impatient as time went on. "I've got too much to do to spend all this time looking for a cat," she grumbled.

"What are you doing?" I asked politely.

"Some of this stuff is going to be donated to museums," she answered. "I have to count it all and type up the lists for the appraisers. You can't imagine how many sets of silverware, crystal, linens, and even Mr. Murdock's old collections of miniature trains there are in this house. I'll be counting for years." She threw up her hands in exasperation.

"It's pretty boring work. I'm really a model, you know."

"Oh, that sounds exciting," I exclaimed. "I thought you were pretty enough to do something like that."

"I modeled cosmetics," she said, waving her hand. "Like lipsticks and nail polish. Miss Murdock's father owns the Beauty Girl Cosmetics Company."

"Oh," I sighed, "I've seen their advertisements in magazines. Their models are always so glamorous." I snapped my fingers. "That's where I've seen you. But why did you stop?"

She looked pleased that I had recognized her, but then a frown passed over her features. "I didn't. Beauty Girl is featuring the country look right now. Mr. Murdock wanted a girl with freckles. He said I was too glamorous. And no one else would hire me because I was too well known as 'The Beauty Girl.' I needed some money. So when Miss Murdock offered me a job as her secretary, I took it. Just temporarily, of course. I didn't know she was going to come to Lexington. I'll never get any modeling jobs here, that's for sure."

We had checked all the upstairs rooms without finding a sign of the missing cat.

"This is Miss Murdock's room," Victoria Presser said, knocking softly on a door on the second floor. Her blouse had come untucked in the search and there was a streak of dust where she had wiped her hand across her cheek.

29

I almost changed my mind about old houses when I glanced in the door. Three of the walls were covered with warm, solid wood paneling, and the molding around the ceiling was beautifully carved. Miss Murdock had been hanging wallpaper on the fourth wall. It was a pretty, old-fashioned flower print. A brightly lit fireplace at one end of the room added to the cozy feeling.

"Any sign of him?" Miss Murdock asked quickly. She sighed when Victoria Presser shook her head. "I suppose you think I am silly," she said, glancing absently at me. "Cats get very attached to their homes. When you move you have to be very careful or else the cat will try to get back to the place where it used to live."

I was silent. I could almost picture the cat trying to walk to New York. No wonder Miss Murdock was so unhappy.

"I'll keep looking," I offered.

"No, dear. It would just be a waste of time. Lucifer is obviously not in the house. Perhaps he'll return when he gets hungry. I'd like you to start working in the library."

Miss Murdock led me back downstairs. We stopped in the kitchen long enough to pick up a supply of rags and polish, then headed to the library. This room was nice, too, although on Saturday I'd been amazed at how dusty it was. It also had a fireplace, a huge stone one that covered one whole wall. The other walls were lined with shelves, and a comfortable-looking chair and a table had been placed by the window, which overlooked a wide stretch of lawn.

"When my grandfather died we hired some people to close up the house and put everything in storage. I'm afraid they didn't do much with the books except throw them in boxes. Some of them are very old. I'll probably sell most of them or donate them, but for now I'd like to see the library as I remember it when I was a child," she said. "Grandfather had a lot of books about trains. That was how my great-grandfather made the family fortune." Miss Murdock chuckled. "I was fascinated by trains, too, when I was a child. I wanted to be an engineer when I grew up."

Miss Murdock demonstrated how to use the polish, which had to be applied and then wiped off with a clean rag. I picked up a rag and started vigorously polishing one shelf after another. The house was quiet except for the clickity-clack of the typewriter coming from the office where Victoria Presser was now doing her work.

Then, just as Miss Murdock turned to leave the room, a huge black cat darted from between two shelves and dashed between my legs. It nearly scared me out of two years' growth, and I really can't afford to lose any height. I am already the shortest girl in my class. But I could have had a heart attack and died right there and Miss Murdock would not have noticed.

"There you are, my bad baby. Where have you been hiding?" Miss Murdock knelt down and

31

stroked the cat happily while I sat on a box waiting for my legs to stop shaking.

Obviously this was the missing Lucifer. But where had he been? Victoria Presser and I had searched this room just a few minutes before.

"This is Lucifer, as you have probably guessed," said Miss Murdock, glancing at me at last. She picked him up and stood holding him. "Lucifer, this is the nice young lady I told you about."

I was beginning to wonder if Mrs. DuPrey's school was worth all of this. Here I was, alone in a spooky mansion with a weird woman who introduced her cat to people and a gardener who watched the house with binoculars. I could see him out of the window, standing half hidden in a clump of trees. I picked up the rag again and started dusting shelves.

"He must have been in there," I said, peering behind the shelf. "There is a hole in the wall back here." I bent down for a closer look.

"It must be some sort of air vent," Miss Murdock said. "I'll have to get a grate to cover it up. Just leave it for now."

She picked up Lucifer and went back to her room. I rubbed and polished the shelves, noting with satisfaction the rich gleam of wood when I had finished. It took quite a while, but at last I was ready to start on the books. I opened several boxes, relieved to see that they were packed more or less in alphabetical order. In a short time I had several shelves filled. I dusted each book carefully before putting it away. The room smelled of old leather and musty paper and ink. I was beginning to enjoy the job. I wished I could stop and browse through the books. Many of them looked interesting.

I reached for another crate when I saw the word "breakable." It was just like the box Miss Murdock had told me not to touch the first day. The top of this crate had come loose and I could easily pry it open. I could not resist a peek. Almost everything was wrapped carefully in paper, but I could see a microscope and test tubes. Miss Murdock had more laboratory equipment than the science lab at school. Why would she need things like that? I wondered.

I heard footsteps and looked up. Frowning slightly when she saw me leaning over the crate, Miss Murdock bustled back in the room. "I expect your parents will be wanting you home for dinner soon," she said. Then she smiled. "My, you have been hard at work. This room is looking nice."

I was pleased at the praise. I had a feeling Miss Murdock wasn't the type to toss around meaning- less compliments. The room was starting to shape up. I could almost imagine myself curled up in front of the fireplace with one of those old books. It was curious. From the outside of the house you would expect to find huge, empty rooms. Yet most of the rooms, while generous in size, did not seem that much larger than those in a normal house.

"I love this room," Miss Murdock said softly. "I used to sit on Grandfather's lap and he would read to me. He was very old-fashioned. Every night he would hold the chair for Grandma to sit. He often talked about how his father had taught him the importance of good manners, but no one cared anymore. It used to drive my parents crazy, I guess, but I didn't mind. That's about all that I can remember about him, that and his reading to me. I could hardly wait to grow up so I could read all these books."

"Did you?"

A brief, sad look passed over her features. "No. My father never got along with Grandfather. Not long after my grandmother died, they had a terrible row. We moved to New York and they never spoke again."

I thought of the poor old man, ending up alone in this huge house. No wonder he had such a reputation for being a grouch before he died.

I was still curious about the lab equipment but I couldn't ask about it without admitting I had been snooping, so I just said good night and promised I'd be back the next day. I didn't see Victoria Presser as I left, but I found Jason waiting by the door just like he had promised.

"I have to put these tools away," he said. "Then I'll go with you."

As we walked back to the toolshed I told him about the crates. "Why do you suppose she has all that lab equipment?" I asked.

"Maybe it's a hobby. I've got a chemistry set," he said, sounding unconcerned.

"It looked like a lot more than hobby equipment," I said. "And she didn't want me to see it."

"Maybe it's a secret hobby," he said. "Maybe she is a witch. Doesn't she have a black cat named Lucifer?"

"Be serious," I said. But I could not help laughing at the image of Miss Murdock riding a broom with Lucifer in her lap. "I think a witch has a big black pot, not test tubes."

Jason hung the rake on a hook in the toolshed and carefully latched the door. I glanced at the woods as I waited. A bright flash of something red glinted in the setting sun. "Hey, what's that?" I asked.

Jason shaded his eyes with his hand. "I don't know. We haven't worked back there yet."

"Let's go see," I said, leading the way. We picked our way through the dense brush that crept over the back lawn from the woods.

"It's a well," Jason exclaimed when we were close enough to see.

It looked like something out of a fairy book, with its colored stones nearly covered with twisting vines. A few days ago it would have been completely hidden by the thick growth, but enough leaves had fallen for the sun to strike its roof and make it visible from the toolshed.

"I wonder if there is any water in it," Jason said, leaning over the edge. "It's too dark to see. Find a stone and I'll toss it in." His voice sounded hollow. He straightened up and I handed him a stone. "There are steps and a rail—like a ladder. Do you

suppose they had to climb down and clean it?" He dropped the rock and a second later we heard a metallic ping.

"Must be dry," Jason said.

"It is so overgrown with vines and brush I'll bet everyone has forgotten it's even there," I said.

"Somebody knows," Jason replied. "The weeds are flattened down around the back. And look. You can see a faint trail leading into the woods."

I was still puzzling over this strange bit of information as we walked back past the toolshed. Mr. Bemiss was bent over, replacing bricks bordering a flower bed next to the driveway. He straightened up and stared at us. The corners of his thin lips turned down in a decidedly unfriendly scowl. "What are you two doing still here? I thought you left fifteen minutes ago."

I spoke quietly before Jason could answer. "We've just been standing here talking." There was something special about the well and discovering it together like that. I didn't want to share it with this grouchy old man.

The look on his face didn't soften. "You two get home. It will be dark in a few minutes. Your parents will worry," he added, with a faint smile that made him look even less friendly.

Mr. Bemiss stood aside to let us pass, but I felt his eyes watching until we reached the street.

"Boy, is he a grump," I said when we were out of hearing distance.

"I think he just doesn't like kids," Jason said.

"But he treats me all right when we're working."

All too quickly we arrived at my house. I waved good-bye and watched as Jason continued up the street. I'd been so busy talking about Mr. Bemiss that I hadn't really found out anything about Jason. Oh well, I thought as I hurried up my front steps. He only walked home with me because there was no one else around. Even a frog was company when you were alone.

FOUR

Can She Bake a Cherry Pie?

Mr. Schuller, the principal of Roosevelt Middle School, had decided that all the sixth-grade girls would take nine weeks of workshop and the boys would take nine weeks of home economics. At the end of the grading period we would switch. To say that my nine weeks of workshop had not been a success would be the understatement of the year. That was how the workshop teacher had tactfully put it in a letter he wrote to my parents. It would have been more accurate to call it a calamity, catastrophe, disaster, or any other terrible word you could think of. At the end of the nine weeks the only thing I had to show for my efforts was one set of crooked bookends. I thought I was pretty lucky to get out of there without killing or maiming anyone, especially myself. Mom and Dad had made a big fuss, pretending the bookends were the most wonderful things they had ever seen. But after a few days Mom put them on the top shelf of the bookcase, where, with a little luck, no one would notice them. I knew she was disappointed. She has great visions of me as a liberated woman. Personally, I was having enough problems being a girl.

I'd worked for Miss Murdock for a whole week now. She had decided to let the books go for a while and instead had me help her hang wallpaper. Amazingly enough, I discovered it was something I could do. Miss Murdock said one afternoon that I had a real "flair" for decorating. Naturally, I was hoping that some of that flair would spill over into cooking and make home economics go a little better than workshop had. But Monday morning, as I stood in the school kitchen, I knew that was only wishful thinking.

"After each lesson you may each take the results home to your families," Mrs. Graham said. "I am sure they will be amazed at your culinary skills." She tucked some stray wisps of hair behind her ears. Mrs. Graham's hair had a mind of its own. Every few seconds a stray curl would pop out as though it were a spring. Her voice was squeaky and her nose twitched when she talked.

"I think Mrs. Graham was probably some kind of rodent in another life," Sue leaned over and whispered.

A giggle escaped my lips, and Mrs. Graham turned her beady eyes toward me. "I fail to see the humor in making a pie crust, Miss Adams."

"Sorry," I said weakly. I looked at my dough and gave a horrified gasp.

Sue Archer was my partner. I liked Sue, but today I would have gladly strangled her. While Mrs. Graham had been instructing us, Sue had eaten half the dough. There was no way the remaining dough would cover the top of the pie.

"If we roll the dough any thinner we will be able to see through it," I wailed.

"Maybe we could put the lattice strips farther apart," Sue offered helpfully. She pulled a candy bar out of her pocket and munched on it while she considered the problem.

The office helper came to the door with a note for Mrs. Graham. She read it quickly and raised her hand.

"I know I can trust you young ladies to continue while I make an important telephone call."

There was a surprised few seconds of silence after she scurried out. I glanced around. Sara and Dawn were partners at the next table. I'd given Sara a sympathetic look when Mrs. Graham paired them off, but Sara had not seemed upset. In fact, they almost seemed to be having a good time. They were talking quietly and every once in a while one of them would laugh. Sara had been practically ignoring me since I started my job, but I was trying not to show how much it hurt. Every time I passed her in the halls I smiled as if nothing had changed.

41

I heard Sara giggle and looked up. She was looking straight at me, and I had the awful feeling I was
the subject of her laughter.

"How do you like working at the Murdock
house?" Sara asked in a loud voice. You could have
heard a pin drop as twelve pairs of eyes zeroed in
on me.

"You're working at the Murdock house?" Sue
squealed.

"I'm helping Miss Murdock move in," I said, as
casually as I could.

"I hear your parents are making you earn the
money for charm school," Dawn said.

I glared at Sara. There was only one place Dawn
could have heard that.

"Jason Whitney works there, too," Sara informed
everyone.

"He's really cute," Missy said. "Do you like
him?"

I shrugged, trying to sound casual. "As a friend,"
I said. "We've been walking home together."

"I'd be scared to work in that creepy house," Sue
said.

"If you got too scared," Dawn said, "you could
just grab something more to eat."

"Hey," I said, though a minute before I'd been
ready to kill Sue myself. "Leave Sue alone. She can't
help it if she gets hungry."

Sue shot me a grateful look. Her face was a bright
pink. "I get depressed when I see how fat I am.
That makes me eat more."

"You ought to go to charm school with Cassie," Dawn told Sue. "You two make a good pair."

Now I felt my face turning crimson. Several girls had gone back to work, trying to ignore the uncomfortable silence. Then, to my surprise, Missy came to my defense.

"I think Mrs. DuPrey's school will be fun. But you are the one who needs it, not Cassie. Evidently Jason doesn't think Cassie needs it, either."

"That's true," Dawn said in a sugar-sweet voice. She turned to me. "I guess he's never seen you in a dress."

Like a fly I stepped right into her web. "I wear jeans to work. So what?"

Dawn smiled. "That's a smart move. That way he won't notice you have legs like an ape."

There I stood, a frog with hairy legs. Sara was bent over, choking with laughter. I bit back angry tears. I didn't know anyone had noticed that my legs were getting hairy. It had been bothering me for a couple of months, but Mom and Dad were kind of funny about things like that. They thought kids tried to grow up too fast. I was going to ask for an electric shaver for Christmas. But the only one I had told how much it bothered me had been Sara. I looked at her, unwilling to believe that she had told something so personal, yet knowing it was true. Smirking, she stared back.

"My mom says if you start shaving too soon it makes the hair grow faster," said Missy comfortingly. "I don't shave mine yet, either."

"You are so blonde it doesn't show. I've been shaving mine for two years," Dawn said. She pulled up her pants leg to show off smooth, hairless legs.

"Don't pay any attention," Missy leaned over and whispered. "Dawn's just jealous because Jason won't pay any attention to her."

I gave her a weak smile. "I'm not scared to work at the Murdock house," I said to change the subject. "But there is a real peculiar gardener there. He's always snooping around. And Miss Murdock is bringing in all kinds of lab equipment. Jason and I can't figure out what's going on."

"A mystery," Missy squealed. "It's just like this book I am reading. It's set in a scary house with a sinister butler. And there's a handsome hero, too."

"Even if there was some kind of mystery, what makes you think *you* could solve it?" Dawn said. Her voice made me think of a snake. "Maybe the great detective can find out who robbed my uncle's house last night," she said to the other girls.

For a minute I forgot my anger. "Your uncle got robbed?"

"Don't you ever listen to the news? His coin collection was stolen, and my aunt lost some jewels. I suppose you are too busy 'working' to know what's going on."

"I hope your pies are ready to pop in the ovens. It's nearly time for the bell, girls," Mrs. Graham squeaked, saving me from having to think up a nasty reply. "If you come back after school I will

44

have them ready for you to take home. Each pie pan is numbered so I will know to whom it belongs."

"You can take my share of pie home," Sue said. She sighed. "Mom wouldn't let me eat it anyway. She's trying to make me lose weight."

I smiled sympathetically as I helped her wipe up our work area. Who cared about Dawn and her uncle, anyway? If her uncle was anything like her it would be hard to feel sorry for him. Dawn was still telling Sara about the robbery, and I could not help hearing.

"The police say it looks like the same burglar who has been doing all these robberies in town lately."

I only half listened to the details as I worked. I had enough mystery of my own. What I had said to Missy was true, even though I liked working for Miss Murdock. But things were happening at that old mansion that made me uneasy. Miss Murdock's lab equipment had disappeared. I had been in almost every room putting things away, and there was no sign of it. And I couldn't shake the feeling that there was something strange about Mr. Bemiss. Every time I turned around it seemed like he was there watching. Even Jason had noticed it. He thought Mr. Bemiss always managed to work where he could watch everyone's comings and goings.

I would have put up with a dozen Mr. Bemisses to be around Miss Presser, or Vicky, as she insisted I call her. She was teaching me beauty secrets after

I finished my work. She showed me how to balance a book on my head to help me walk gracefully, and Saturday afternoon she had given me a manicure, even though Mom had said it was much too red for my age and made me take off the polish. And of course there was Jason. He continued to walk home with me, although I had discovered it was not on his way at all.

After school I stopped in the home economics room to collect the cherry pie. In spite of a skimpy crust, it didn't look too bad. I raced home as fast as I could without dropping it. There was something I had to do before I went to work.

I put the pie in the cupboard and ran to the bathroom. Tomorrow, I vowed, I would wear a dress to school. And under it would be the smoothest legs you ever saw. I wasn't sure where Mom kept her electric razor, but Dad's supplies were in the cabinet. Carefully I applied the cream and started. I was so intent on the job I didn't hear Danny until he opened the door and burst into the room.

"Haven't you ever heard of knocking?" I screamed.

"I didn't know you were—haven't you ever heard of asking permission?" he said with a crafty look. "I'll bet Dad wouldn't like you using his razor."

I dabbed at the blood dripping from a cut. He was right, of course. But I hadn't wanted to take the chance Mom would say I was too young.

"You'd better not tell," I said, trying to look

fierce. "And what are you doing home, anyway? You're supposed to be at Arnold's."

"I just stopped to leave my books and pick up my football." He paused. "I won't tell. But if I do you a favor, you should do one for me."

"Like what?"

"Like take me with you to the Murdock house. I want to see it. Arnold will be purple with envy."

"Green," I said absently.

"Not Arnold. He'll turn purple," Danny said. "Come on. Will you take me? I won't get in the way."

"I'm working, remember? And I don't know if Miss Murdock would like it."

"You could say you have to baby-sit me for a few minutes. I'll look at the house, and then go to Arnold's."

I hesitated. I knew Danny too well. If I didn't let him come with me he would be mean enough to tattle. "All right," I agreed. "But just look at the house and leave."

"It's a deal," he said, looking triumphant.

Miss Murdock was pleasant when I stumbled over an explanation about Danny. "Come in," she said, wiping a speck of paint off her glasses. "You can help your sister."

"He won't be staying that long," I said hastily.

"This is a terrific house," Danny said. "Would you mind if I looked around? I promise I won't touch anything."

"Why, of course," Miss Murdock said, falling for

Danny's innocent look. "I would show you around myself but the roofers are waiting to talk to me. Maybe Miss Presser could go with you."

Vicky's desk was nearly buried under books and papers. She smiled when Miss Murdock made her request, but not before I saw an irritated look pass over her face. Who could blame her? I wouldn't want to take a ten-year-old pest on a tour, either.

"I'll go finish the library. I've only got one more box of books to put away," I said.

"Come on," Vicky snapped at Danny. I looked at her in surprise. It wasn't like her to be so impatient. She didn't really have any reason to dislike Danny. But Danny trotted eagerly after her and I heard him asking a dozen questions as they walked down the hall. I was surprised. Maybe he really was interested in old houses.

I went to work in the library, glancing out the window from time to time at Miss Murdock. She was still talking to the roofers. One of them was big and blonde. His arms were huge, like he worked out a lot. He was doing most of the talking. The other man was thinner and he had a snake tattooed on his lower arm. He leaned against an old pickup truck filled with ladders and tools. "Bob and Dave Construction" it said in new-looking letters on the side of the cab. Mr. Bemiss was digging in the flower bed nearby, his usual scowl in place, but he seemed very interested in the conversation. He inched closer as he worked, as though he was trying to listen.

The blonde man leaned closer and said something to Miss Murdock and she laughed. He's flirting with her, I thought in amazement.

I had nearly finished filling up the shelves from the last carton of books when Miss Murdock came back in the house. She paused in front of the hall mirror to pat her hair. As she passed the doorway to the library she glanced in. "This was a big job, and you have done it beautifully."

Praise is nice, but it is also uncomfortable. I never know what to say when someone gives me a compliment. So usually I end up ducking my red face and mumbling thank you and then trying to change the subject. That was exactly what I did then.

"Can the roof be fixed?" I asked.

Miss Murdock nodded. "It will be a little noisy here for a while. Part of the rafters will have to be replaced. I'm afraid Grandfather became very neglectful. He waited until the roof was practically falling in before he hired Bob Henshaw. The job was only half done when Grandfather passed away. I was glad to find Bob has time to finish it now." Miss Murdock sat down in the easy chair and stroked Lucifer, who had promptly hopped into her lap. She looked out the window at the blonde man, who was loading a ladder onto the truck.

"Bob lived just up the street when I stayed with my grandfather as a child. This land was mostly open then, just a few farms here and there. There weren't too many other children around, so he came over to play once in a while. I haven't seen him for more than twenty years."

Danny and Vicky walked into the room and Miss Murdock reverted to her usual reserved self. But just for a second I had seen another side of her, a warm and very human side.

Danny was still chattering away, but Vicky seemed in better spirits. "I hope you enjoyed the tour," she said to Danny. "I have to get back to work now."

"I won't be here for dinner tonight, Vicky," Miss Murdock said. "I hope you won't mind eating alone. I will be dining with Mr. Henshaw."

"No problem," Vicky said cheerfully. When Miss Murdock turned away Vicky gave me a knowing wink. It did seem strange for Miss Murdock to have a date.

The women walked out together and I glared at Danny. "All right. You saw what you wanted. Now scram."

"I know I promised," Danny said seriously. "But I need to talk to you. There is something very strange about this house."

FIVE

A Secret Room and a Strange Conversation

"The only thing strange about this house is you being in it, buzzard bait," I said. Then I noticed his face. He was deadly serious.

"What do you mean?" I asked more kindly.

"Well, for one thing, all the rooms on this floor seem too small. Upstairs they seem about right, but not down here."

"I noticed that," I said. "I suppose it is because the walls are so thick."

"No, it's more than that. I think there is another room somewhere. A hidden room."

"You've been watching too many movies," I retorted.

"All right, smarty. Where is the room with the octagonal window?"

That stopped me. I ran through the rooms in my mind. "I don't know," I said slowly. "Did you see a room with a lot of laboratory equipment?"

Danny shook his head. "Why would there be a laboratory?"

I told him about the crates of test tubes I'd seen.

"Maybe they are in the hidden room. But why would anyone have a secret laboratory?" Danny said. "Unless they were making something bad, like drugs."

"Don't be silly," I said. "Miss Murdock's not that sort of person. Go on to Arnold's house like you promised." I couldn't help thinking Danny's theory made sense, although I wasn't about to admit it.

I was just finishing the library when Miss Murdock came back and handed me my first week's wages. I had worked two hours after school every night and half a day on Saturday, but instead of handing me twenty-eight dollars she handed me thirty. "Here is a little extra for doing such a nice job," she smiled.

"Thank you," I said, feeling guilty for my thoughts a few minutes before. I stuffed the bills in my pocket. It was a terrific feeling, having earned that much by myself. In two more weeks I would have more than enough for Mrs. DuPrey's school.

To my surprise Danny was sitting on the steps waiting for me when I came outside. He jumped up and followed me as I walked toward the street.

"What are you doing still here?" I asked.

Danny shrugged. "I told Arnold's mother I wanted to meet you. I didn't feel like playing football tonight. That's all Arnold ever wants to do."

"I thought you liked football."

"I do, but not every minute."

"I guess it's like Sara and me. We've been friends since the first grade, but it's like we've outgrown each other."

"By the way, thanks for taking me with you," Danny said. "I wouldn't really have told about you using Dad's razor."

"Why didn't you just ask me, then?" I said.

"Because you wouldn't have taken me. Ever since Mom went back to work you act like you hate me."

"I don't hate you," I said. I thought about Mr. Wilson and the paper boy. The paper boy was a pain, but Mr. Wilson had treated him like a horrible criminal. Was I taking my anger out on Danny? Danny was a pain, too, but he really wasn't as terrible as I'd been treating him.

"Cassie, wait up," Jason called. While we waited for Jason to put away his tools Danny studied the house with a slight frown.

"Danny thinks there might be a hidden room in the house," I said when Jason caught up to us.

"I wish there was some way to find out for sure," Danny said.

"What makes you think that?" asked Jason.

Jason listened thoughtfully as we explained. "You might be right," he said. "I think a lot of old houses were made with hidden rooms." He was quiet for a minute and then he snapped his fingers. "I know how we might be able to find out. I did a project at my old school about the early history of Chicago, and the librarian showed me a lot of neat books. I'll bet Lexington's library would have the same sort of information."

"I could go after dinner," I said.

Danny looked unhappy. "It was my idea."

"Why don't we all go?" Jason said. "I could meet you there. It will go faster if we all look."

Mom was already putting dinner on the table when we walked in the door. I washed my hands and hurried to help. "Miss Murdock paid me for last week. Look," I said, pulling the money out of my pocket.

"Put it in your bank so you don't lose it," she said absently. Then she looked at Dad. "What happened to your face?"

Dad was wearing two tiny Band-Aids, one on his chin and one on his cheek. "I wanted to shave before dinner, but I guess my blade was duller than I thought," he said.

I swallowed and glanced at Danny, but he wasn't going to tell. He was looking at the evening paper like he was really interested.

"Maybe you should switch to a different brand," Mom said.

"There was another robbery," Danny informed us. "Somebody's coin collection. It was worth twenty thousand dollars."

"I'll bet that was Dawn's uncle." I grabbed the paper.

"There have been an awful lot of robberies lately," Mom said. "I'm glad we don't have anything worth stealing."

"I heard about that." Dad glanced at the paper. "The radio said the police were baffled. Usually when there is a robbery the thieves try to sell the loot. But none of the stolen items has turned up."

The dinner conversation was mostly about the robberies. I ate quickly, hardly taking time to enjoy Mom's chicken and noodles.

"I have to do some work at the library after dinner," I said as I scraped up the last bite.

"I want to go, too," Danny said. "I need a book to read."

"As long as you are not too long," Dad said. "I want you back home by eight o'clock."

"We have a surprise for dessert." Mom cut into my pie and passed it around.

Dad took a bite. "Mmmm. The crust is a little skimpy, but it's delicious."

"Cassie made it," Danny said. "We might all get sick and die tonight." He made a gagging sound and pretended to choke.

So much for being nice. "If we do, it will be from getting too close to you, dinosaur breath."

"Or looking at your witch face."

"Please," Mom said. "Let's finish our meal in peace. Cassie, the pie is very good."

I stood up to clear the table, but Mom waved her hand. "Go on to the library. Dad and I will take care of the dishes."

That made me feel a little guilty. But research is research, I told myself as I marched out the door, still angry at Danny.

"I was just kidding about the pie," Danny said, hurrying to keep up.

The library is only a few blocks from our house. It is a low brick building right next to the school. Still ignoring Danny, I went in and looked around for a table. Sometimes they are hard to get because a lot of high-school kids come to the library to do their homework in the evenings. But Jason was already there saving a table. He had several thick books stacked up in front of him.

"I can't find anything," he whispered. "The house is mentioned in this book." He gestured to the top of the stack. "But nothing about a hidden room."

"How did you get here so soon?" I asked. "We ate as fast as we could."

Jason shrugged. "I made myself a sandwich and ate it on the way to the library."

"Your mom lets you just eat a sandwich for dinner?"

"She isn't home. She works at night at the Big Basket grocery store."

Danny and I exchanged a look. Here we were griping because our mother got home at five. How would we feel if we were alone all evening?

"What did you find out?" I asked, sitting down in the chair beside him.

"I haven't had time to look through all of these

books. But this one says that the house was built in 1870 by a man named Joseph Murdock. He was a big industrialist, into building railroads and that sort of thing."

I picked up another book from the stack and leafed through it. "Here's something." I read quickly. "This book says Mr. Murdock was a very private sort of person. No one knew very much about him. That must be Miss Murdock's great-grandfather. His son, Miss Murdock's grandfather, lived in the house, too. She said she visited her grandfather there when she was young."

"You'd think there would be something about the house having a hidden room if it were true," Jason said.

Danny shook his head. "I'm sure it's there."

I thought about the window that made me think of the cyclops. "He's right," I said thoughtfully. "We can figure out where it must be. On that side of the house there are four rooms, and there are eight windows, counting the octagon. Miss Presser's office is in the back and it has two windows. There are two in the front room. In the middle are the music room and the library. I think there are two windows in the music room, but there is only one in the library. And none of the rooms has an octagonal window."

"Then the secret room must be between the library and the music room," Danny chimed in.

"There isn't any door between them," I said. "I've been working in the library a lot."

"Maybe there is a movable bookcase," Jason said. "I saw that in a movie once."

I shook my head. "I doubt it. I dusted and worked on those shelves. They are heavy. Lucifer found some sort of air vent. But it's on the wrong side of the room, and anyway it's much too small for a human to squeeze through."

Danny walked over to the librarian's desk and stood earnestly talking for a few minutes. When he came back he was grinning. "The librarian says that the County Historical Society knows about old houses. I got the name of a woman who might be able to tell us something."

"Good thinking," Jason said. Danny grinned, pleased with the praise.

"We won't have a chance to go until Saturday. I'll call her and see if we can talk to her then," I said.

"I'm really glad we moved to Lexington," Jason said on the way home. "I didn't think I would like it at first. Mom and I always lived in big towns before. I guess I thought living here would be dull."

"Why did you move here?" I asked.

"A friend of hers gave her the job managing the grocery store at night so she can attend college. But it's just for a year," Jason answered. "Then she will be a teacher." I heard a proud note creep into his voice when he talked about his mother. "It gets kind of lonesome, but it will be worth it when she graduates."

"Let's walk by the Murdock house," I said. "I'd like to look at the windows again."

"What do you suppose Miss Murdock is doing in the secret room?" Jason asked.

"I don't know," I said. "I hope it isn't anything bad. She really seems nice."

We walked up the street along the woods. Far up at the corner a streetlight burned, casting a ghostly glow. I shivered and walked a little faster. We passed a car parked on the dark street. A few steps farther Danny suddenly stopped.

"Who is that?" he whispered. I saw them at the same time, two dark figures standing at the edge of the woods.

Jason took my arm and pulled me back into the shadows. The two men had not seen us and continued talking. I recognized one voice immediately. It was Mr. Bemiss.

"I think we ought to call it off," the other man was saying.

"Just a few more days," Mr. Bemiss growled. "I know I am right. As long as those kids don't mess everything up."

"Keep an eye on them," the first man said sharply.

Mr. Bemiss sighed. "I am. But you know how snoopy kids are. It could be bad for them if they got in the way. But we can't blow it now."

"All right," the first man said. "But I want results. How about the woman?"

"I don't know yet. That's why I need more time."

The first man grunted a reply and started back to his car.

He passed within inches of where we were crouched behind some bushes, but by now the darkness was so complete he did not notice us. We held our breath, afraid to move until we heard the car door slam and the motor start. Jason peered through the inky night, but Mr. Bemiss had disappeared, also.

"I think they've both gone," he said, standing up. "Why would Mr. Bemiss be meeting someone in the dark like that?"

My heart was still pounding, but Danny sounded almost cheerful. "Because he's a crook," Danny said. "And he is going to do something awful."

"Like what?" Jason's face looked ghostly against the blackness of the night.

"Maybe Miss Murdock makes drugs in her secret laboratory, and Mr. Bemiss sells them," Danny said.

"Miss Murdock doesn't seem like that sort of person. And Miss Presser is super nice. Wouldn't she know if her boss was a drug dealer?" I asked.

"Then you give me a better solution," Danny demanded.

Suddenly a twig cracked, shattering the eerie silence in the woods surrounding us. I was blinded by the glare of a light shining directly in my eyes. But I didn't need to see to recognize that voice.

"What in blazes are you kids doing here?" Mr. Bemiss asked in a sinister, cold voice.

SIX

Some Helpful
Information

For an instant all three of us stood frozen as though we had become one of the giant trees in the woods, rooted, unable to move. My mind was the only thing working, and it was whirling in panic. How long had he been standing there listening?

Danny found his voice first. "We were just walking home from the library and I dropped my lucky coin."

"In the bushes?"

"Well, I was flipping it in the air," Danny demonstrated with his hands. "Maybe I could find it if you would shine your light. I hate to go anywhere without my lucky coin."

My mouth was dry, making it hard to swallow. Mr. Bemiss wasn't buying the story.

"Dad gave it to him for his birthday. It means a lot to him," I managed to choke out.

Mr. Bemiss aimed the light at the bushes and

played the beam over the ground. I saw a glint of silver as the light passed over a clump of weeds. "That's it," Danny shouted. "Gee, thanks. I'm so glad you came along with your light."

"You shouldn't be out here in the dark."

Jason found his voice. "We know. Cassie's dad is probably already out looking for us."

"Get going then," growled Mr. Bemiss, releasing us.

We didn't wait for a change of mind. We raced up the street, not slowing until we reached the corner and the safety of the dim streetlight.

"That was good thinking, Danny," I said, gasping for breath after our run. "But how did you know there would be a coin there?"

Danny grinned. "Because I tossed it there a second before."

"Do you suppose he heard us talking?" Jason asked. We turned down the road by the Murdock mansion, heading for home.

"Look at that," Danny whispered, grabbing my arm. A ghostly glow drifted quickly past the octagonal window, then faded away.

"That's the window in the hidden room," Danny said. "Maybe there really are ghosts."

"There are no such things as ghosts," I said automatically, wishing I was as sure as I sounded.

"If only the window wasn't so high. Then we could peek in," Jason said.

"Maybe it's only Miss Murdock," Danny offered.

"No, she went out with Mr. Henshaw, the roofer," I told him.

"It's not Miss Presser, either," Danny said, pointing. Her office window was brightly lit and I could see her sitting at her desk.

"Do you think we should tell her?" Jason asked.

I shook my head. "What would we say? That we saw a ghost? Besides, it's gone now, and if we don't get home our dad might be really out looking for us."

We waved good-bye to Jason, and Danny and I slipped in the back door. "Don't say anything to Mom and Dad," I whispered. "They might not let me go back to the house."

"Maybe that's not such a bad idea." Danny looked serious.

"No," I whispered fiercely. "I need the money. And Vicky is teaching me all kinds of neat things."

Danny's look told me what he thought of that, but he shrugged.

"Where have you two been?" Mom said as she came into the kitchen. "I was beginning to get worried."

"Sorry we are late," I said. "It took longer than I thought."

"Don't let it happen again," Mom said. "You heard your father tell you to be home by eight o'clock."

I reached in the cookie jar and pulled out a handful of cookies. Then I poured two glasses of milk.

65

Dad walked into the room just as we sat down at the kitchen table. "I heard something about your Miss Murdock today. Her family owns the Beauty Girl Cosmetics Company, or at least her father does."

"Vicky Presser told me that," I said.

"Did you know that was why her grandfather had a falling-out with her father? Seems the old man didn't think cosmetics was a suitable occupation for a man. He wanted his son to take over the family business. They had words and the grandfather didn't speak to him for years. That's probably why the old man was so bitter and lonely. But he must have loved his granddaughter, and that's why he left her the house."

"That's kind of sad," I said.

Dad nodded. "I'm surprised Miss Murdock isn't part of her father's company."

An image of Miss Murdock crossed my mind. "I don't think she's into makeup."

"Miss Presser is," Danny said, stuffing the last of his cookie in his mouth. "She wears gobs."

"She does not," I said. "She says if you know how to apply it you can enhance your natural good features." I sighed. "Of course, it helps if you have some good features to enhance."

"You have a lot of good features," Dad said, kissing the top of my head.

I was going to say, name one, but I pressed my lips closed. That remark would only get me a pep talk. It was nice of him, in a way. I mean, I really didn't want him to say yeah, I have noticed how homely you are. But when I looked in the mirror I could see the truth.

Danny had gone to his room. I stopped on the way to my own room and tapped on his door. He was sitting on the bed reading a book. It was the one he had checked out of the library so Mom and Dad didn't get suspicious.

He looked up and said, "This is pretty good. It's all about some kids that capture some kidnappers."

"How do you know that already? You just started reading."

"I read the end, of course."

"Now you've spoiled the book."

"I have to look at the end to see if I want to read it all the way through," Danny explained.

Right then I decided there were two kinds of people in the world: those who read the ends of books first, and those who like to be surprised. Just that one thing could tell you a lot about a person. I wondered which kind Jason was.

I noticed a small carving on Danny's table, different from the one I'd seen before. "Where did you get this?" I asked, picking it up. The figure was a tiny raccoon peeping mischievously around a log.

"You promise you won't laugh?" Danny asked.

"Why would I laugh?"

Danny shrugged. "Because I made it."

"You?"

"With the penknife Dad gave me for my birthday. I had this piece of wood and I was going to see how good my knife could cut. Then all of a sudden it was like I could see an animal waiting to come out. I've got more," he added, opening a drawer.

I looked at Danny's menagerie of animals. A few were crude and I figured they must have been his first attempts. I could almost see how his skill had improved as he practiced.

"I think you might be a famous artist someday," I said at last.

Danny beamed. "Thanks, Cassie. But I just do it for fun. I'm going to be an astronaut when I grow up."

"Not me," I said. "I'll keep my feet right on the ground where they belong."

"Wouldn't you like to go to the moon, or even Mars?" Danny said. "I think it would be so exciting. Maybe I'll discover a new world someday."

I shook my head. "You can send me a picture. You'll know where to find me. Right here on the good old Earth."

"I will," Danny said. "You just wait and see. I'll send you a picture of me shaking hands with the slime people of Venus, and you can show it to all your friends."

It is hard to figure people out. Here was Danny, who reads the ends of books first and knows exactly what he wants to do with his life when he is only ten years old, and yet he has the imagination to create something like the deer and the raccoon.

"You are a weird kid, Danny," I said. "But I like you."

"I like you, too," Danny said, with a surprised look on his face.

I called Mrs. Endslow, the woman from the historical society, to make an appointment for Saturday. I expected her to be pretty historical herself—a stuffy old lady, prim and proper and maybe a little on the crabby side. But over the phone, Mrs. Endslow seemed warm, sweet, and best of all, willing to talk to us.

We waited impatiently for the week to end, but finally it was Saturday. The three of us walked over to her house together. It was miserably cold outside. Our breath came out in little puffs of steam when we talked. I hadn't been able to find my winter mittens although I had searched through all my drawers. Vaguely I seemed to remember that I had lost them at the end of last winter. Danny, of course, found his right away, but I noticed that Jason wasn't wearing any either. By the time we reached our destination my fingers were ready to crack with cold and my nose was dripping. It is hard to be glamorous any time, but in twenty-degree weather it is impossible.

"I didn't think it was this far," I said.

"I just hope we didn't walk over here for nothing," Jason grumbled.

"I heard we are going to get some snow in a couple of days," Danny said cheerfully. "I can hardly wait."

"The only thing that makes me like winter is ice-skating," I said. "The town freezes over the tennis courts in the park so people can skate. Danny and I go all the time. Would you like to go with us sometime?"

The minute I asked I wished I could take it back. What if he thought I was asking him for a date? It was pretty obvious the idea made him uncomfortable. He looked embarrassed and several long seconds went by before he answered.

"I would like to go," he said finally. "But I'd look dumb. I've never been ice-skating. Anyway, I don't have any skates."

Relief flooded over me. I hadn't considered the possibility that he didn't know how. "It's really easy," I said. "And fun. My dad has some skates that might fit you. His feet are small and these are too small even for him. Danny and I could teach you."

"Sure," Danny said. "And you don't have to worry about people laughing if you fall down. Everyone does once in a while."

"I'd like to go sometime," Jason said shyly.

"Hey, we're here," Danny said, checking the house numbers. We were standing in front of a neat little cottage with a white fence. A lady was peeking through the curtains, as though she were waiting for us.

"Hurry, quick, and come in before you freeze," Mrs. Endslow said, throwing open the door before we even knocked. She took our coats and ushered us into a cheery kitchen. I liked her instantly. Her

70

eyes were a bright blue and the little laugh lines around them crinkled nicely when she smiled. It made her look a lot younger than her snow-white hair suggested. She looked like her name should have been Mrs. Claus. I wouldn't have been surprised to see a room full of elves making toys.

We sat at a table covered with bright red and white checks while she heated milk for hot chocolate.

"I've been thinking about the house all day," she said. "I hope I can answer your questions. Of course, I wasn't born yet when the house was built, although I may look it," she said with a twinkle. "But I did work there for a time when I was young. The first Mr. Murdock was quite old, but he still lived in the house with his son, who was Miss Murdock's grandfather. Her grandmother ran the house and that's who hired me. No one saw very much of the old man."

"Was there anything strange about the house?" I asked.

She gave me a sharp look. "I worked in the kitchen, so I didn't get into the rest of the house very much. The other servants were always telling stories about old Mr. Murdock, though. It seems he was pretty strange."

"What kind of stories?" Danny asked.

"Well, I guess he got quite eccentric as he got older. He was a confirmed recluse, that I know. But his wife loved to entertain. Whenever there was company Mr. Murdock would simply disappear."

71

"Disappear?" Jason repeated.

"He walled off a part of the library, sort of a little office, where he would just go until the company was gone."

"It must not have been very secret," I said, feeling disappointed. "Do you know how he got into the secret room?" I asked.

"Oh, I think there was some sort of sliding panel," Mrs. Endslow said as she poured four steaming mugs of hot chocolate and sat down.

I stared across the table at Danny and Jason. Had we been playing a silly game, making a mystery where none existed?

"There was one thing," Mrs. Endslow said slowly. "I had almost forgotten about this, but something very peculiar happened one day while I was working."

"What was it?" Danny asked eagerly.

"There was a fire in the kitchen. Not a very serious one, but everyone had to leave the house very quickly. Young Mr. Murdock was out of town and Mrs. Murdock was frantic. No one could find the old man. Of course they checked the hidden room, but it was empty. We knew he hadn't left by the front door because it was locked from the inside, and if he had left by the back door we would have seen him from the kitchen."

"Maybe he climbed out a window," Jason suggested.

"I suppose he could have, but it seemed highly unlikely. Anyway, we were all gathered out on the lawn and Mrs. Murdock was carrying on something awful, and suddenly—old Mr. Murdock just appeared as calm as you please."

"From where?" I asked.

"We never knew. He just strolled across the lawn and wouldn't say a word about it. Mr. Murdock didn't seem very surprised when he came back and heard about it, so I suspected that he knew how old Mr. Murdock did it. But our cook, who was a silly thing, started to tell some wild story about the hidden room, that the old man could appear or disappear at will. She hinted at sinister magic going on, or worse. I left soon after but I heard that they finally had to fire her for spreading such wild stories."

"That's pretty interesting," I said.

"Well, I'm not sure if it's important now. I believe Miss Murdock's grandmother remodeled the house after the old man died. The hidden room might not even be there now."

"You've been a big help," I said as I carried our mugs to the sink.

"Oh, I hope so, dear," she said, smiling. "Come again sometime. I don't get much company anymore and I do like to visit."

"We will," we promised as we buttoned our coats.

"She was really nice," I remarked as we started home.

"She was," Jason agreed. "It looks like Danny was right about the hidden room, even if it's not so secret. But we still don't have any idea what is going on."

Danny said, "I'd like to find that room and peek in."

"If she is making drugs that could be dangerous," Jason said, looking worried.

"Well," Danny said cheerfully, "that means we will have to be extra careful."

SEVEN

The Secret Room

It was nearly dinner time when we left Mrs. Endslow's house. My stomach rumbled with hunger pains. "Will your mother be upset if you are late?" I asked Jason.

"She's at work. Grocery stores are busy on Saturdays."

"Who fixes your dinner?" I asked.

"Mom cooks something and then I heat it up for myself," he said.

"That must be terrific," said Danny. "You can eat watching television. Mom will never let us do that."

Jason's face told me eating alone most nights wasn't terrific at all. "Mom never let me watch television during dinner when my dad was home."

"Do you ever see your father?" I asked.

"Not very often. He lives in Chicago. I might go visit him next summer," Jason answered.

"Do you miss him?" Danny asked.

Jason shrugged. "Yeah. We got along pretty well. My mom's great, too," he added quickly. "I guess they just weren't too great together."

"Why don't you eat with us tonight?" I said. "Mom won't mind. We have friends over all the time." I didn't add that we had to check first if it was all right. Maybe Mom would understand that this was kind of an emergency. "Come on," I said, insisting. "You are eating with us."

Mom was just dishing up a big pot of spaghetti when we walked in the back door. She raised her eyebrows a little, but she gave Jason a welcoming smile.

One of Mom's pet rules is about dinner. The television is turned off and everyone sits at the table. Sara never liked to eat at our house because her family eats on little trays while they watch television. I glanced at Jason to see if he looked uncomfortable, but he seemed to be really enjoying himself. He talked easily with Dad and complimented Mom several times on the meal.

After dinner Jason helped wash the dishes. "I noticed the piano when I came in. Do you play it?" he asked me.

"Cassie plays very well," Mom said. "Why don't you play something for Jason before he goes home?"

"Mom!" I exclaimed. I could feel the redness creeping up to my ears.

"Don't let her kid you," Danny said. "She does play well."

Jason looked through my music. " 'Für Elise.' I like that one."

"You know it?"

He grinned. "Sure. My mom makes me take piano, too. Got any duets?"

Before I knew what was happening the whole family was gathered around, and Jason and I played several numbers. After a while I forgot my embarrassment as our hands flew over the keys.

"That was great," Dad said when we reluctantly stopped.

"And," Mom said, with a smile, "Cassie managed to get in a badly needed practice session."

Later that night, Mom came to my room to say good night. Dad had left to drive Jason back to his house. "I'm sorry I didn't ask first," I said. "But I kept thinking about him going back to a cold, dark house all alone."

"I understand," Mom said. "It was a nice thing to do. But don't make it a habit without asking."

"I won't."

Mom looked around my room. "What happened to all this organization you were going to learn? It is hard to imagine how one person can make such a mess, let alone live in it," she said, shaking her head. "Sleep now, if you can find your bed. But first thing tomorrow I want this cleaned up."

I nodded. It wasn't that I didn't want to have a

neat room. I had even made that my New Year's resolution. I had made a little book with columns where I could give myself stars for good behavior and checks for bad. I had headed the columns with things like "Being nice to Danny," "Cleaning room," and "Doing homework on time." At the end of two weeks the checks had outnumbered the stars so much I got discouraged and tucked the book in the back of a drawer.

Danny stuck his head in the door the next morning just as I started cleaning. "This will take you a week," he said cheerfully. "Want some help?"

"I like it this way," I lied. "Everything is handy."

"You need to keep week-old bread crusts under your bed?" Danny asked. He pointed to the plate sticking out from under the foot of the bed. "Or is that to feed the rats?"

Danny's room is always disgustingly neat. But I wasn't about to have my little brother teach me how to keep my room. A person has to have some pride.

"Do you realize what a boring world it would be if everyone kept their rooms neat?" I said. I scraped a few things off the end of my bed so I could sit down.

"Why would it be boring?" Danny asked, laughing.

"If everyone kept their rooms neat, people like you wouldn't have anything to brag about. The world needs people like me."

"Now all you have to do is convince Mom and

Dad," Danny said as he left. He was still laughing. "Have fun."

The sneaker I picked up and threw missed Danny and hit the door with a thud. I could still hear him laughing as he walked down the hall. I didn't care. I'd just noticed that it was my favorite purple tennis shoe. It had been missing for two weeks.

I worked on my room almost all day. It gave me a chance to think about everything that had happened in the past few days. The first question was the conversation we had overheard. What was Mr. Bemiss reluctant to call off? Maybe he had been talking about a shipment of drugs. And if that was true, poor Vicky might be in danger. What if she accidentally found the secret room and found out what they were doing? And what connection did the ghost lights have to all of this? Late that afternoon I had a clean room—and a headache from all that thinking. I still hadn't figured anything out. But I was doubly determined to search for the hidden room.

School the next day seemed to drag on forever. I was anxious to get out and start my search. I couldn't even enjoy the day with Mr. Taylor, my favorite substitute. Ordinarily everyone gives substitutes a hard time. But not Mr. Taylor. He was young and so handsome that half the girls in the room had a crush on him. But the boys liked him even more. Mr. Taylor had been a pilot in the Air Force, and flying was still his first and greatest love.

One way or another, Mr. Taylor worked flying into the lessons. For math we might figure out how long it took to fly somewhere at different speeds. For social studies we might talk about what countries we would fly over going in a certain direction, and for science we might talk about weather patterns. And any of those subjects might get him started talking for hours.

"Where is the safest place to be in a plane that crashes?" Charles asked.

Everyone knew why he had asked that. Charles was flying to California with his parents over the Christmas holidays. It was obvious Charles was not too thrilled with the idea.

"How about home in bed?" Dawn asked. "Shivering under the covers."

Charles tried to laugh, although his face was red. "I'd rather be there than in an airplane."

Sara was snickering behind her hand at Charles's obvious embarrassment. Funny how I'd never noticed her mean spirit before. Mr. Taylor launched a long talk about the safety of planes as opposed to cars. I could tell it wasn't helping Charles feel one bit better. His face was still red and he looked like he wished he had never brought up the subject. I thought I understood. It was probably like sitting in a dark room watching a really creepy movie. Then you hear the floor creak behind you. You can tell yourself not to be silly, that there could not possibly be a monster creeping through the dark kitchen. But there is just that tiny shred of doubt that keeps you from going to check. I thought Charles probably felt that way about flying. No amount of assurance was going to erase that tiny question.

"I wish someone would staple Dawn's mouth shut," I told Missy as we got our lunches out of our lockers.

Sara walked by and overheard. "She was just joking," she said.

"It wasn't funny," I said.

"I thought it was," Sara said defiantly.

That's when I noticed the sweater Sara was wearing. I'd seen it before. On Dawn. It was obvious that they were getting to be pretty good friends. We were still standing there when Dawn came around the corner.

"Well, if it isn't the girl detective," she said. "Have you shaved your legs yet?"

"Have you shaved your lip?" I asked sweetly. "If you did maybe it wouldn't flap around so much."

I walked away before she could answer. Even though I was beginning to see what kind of person Sara really was, it still hurt. I was glad when Missy asked me to eat at her table. Sara and Dawn sat across the room and glared at me all through lunch.

After school I hurried home to drop off my schoolbooks. When I opened the front door I found Danny on the couch, asleep. I was standing there staring at him, wondering if I should wake him or not, when I heard a sound in the kitchen. Before I could react, Mom strolled into the living room balancing a cup of coffee and a sandwich.

"You scared me," I gasped. "I thought you were a burglar or something."

"I'm sorry," Mom whispered, putting down the coffee cup. "They called me at work to come and get Danny. I think he just has the flu, but Mrs. Robert didn't want to watch him when he was sick. She was afraid Arnold would get it."

"Won't you get in trouble at work?"

"My boss was very understanding. I'm not sure he would be if this happened very often, but this time it couldn't be helped."

"I'd better get to work myself," I said, recovering from my surprise.

"How are you doing?" Mom asked.

"Great," I answered. "I've got over half what I need right now."

"I meant how are you doing personally? Is it too hard on you, working every afternoon like this? Your father and I have been very impressed with how hard you've been working. I guess we didn't realize how important it was to you. If it would help we would be willing to give you the rest of the money."

"No, I like working," I said, realizing it was true. "It makes me feel good to be earning money by myself."

"That is a good feeling, isn't it?" she said with a smile. I looked at her in surprise. I had resented

her going back to work. But suddenly I understood. Right before my eyes she changed from Mom into a real person with feelings not so different from my own.

"You are growing up," she said. She sounded proud, but maybe just a little bit sad. And suddenly I understood that, too. "I'm not all that grown up," I said. "I still haven't figured out how to keep my room clean."

Jason was raking leaves when I arrived at the Murdock house. I walked over to say hello before I went into the house.

"I've been watching Mr. Bemiss," he said. "But all he has done is work."

"He's a good gardener," I admitted. The yard looked better every time I saw it. Now that all the overgrown bushes were cleared away and the walks repaired and neatly trimmed, the house looked brighter, less gloomy. I could almost picture what it must have looked like years before.

Even Mr. Bemiss looked brighter. He came around the corner of the house with a rake propped over his shoulder, whistling an off-key version of "Old McDonald Had a Farm." He nodded in my direction. "Good afternoon, young lady."

"I was just looking at the yard," I mumbled nervously. "It is really starting to look nice."

He pushed the battered hat he always wore back on his head and looked around with satisfaction.

"It is, isn't it? But I couldn't have done it without my good helper." He actually smiled at Jason.

From the roof came the sound of hammers. Mr. Bemiss squinted up at the roofers and all traces of his smile disappeared. "We'd better get to work," he told Jason gruffly.

Mr. Henshaw's truck was parked on the drive in front of the house. He gave me a friendly wave as I walked to the door. "Miss Murdock left for a while, but I think Vicky is home," he called down.

Vicky looked tired when she opened the door. "Miss Murdock's out getting her hair done," she said as I followed her to her office. "She has another date with Bob Henshaw tonight."

I thought that sounded kind of nice, but Vicky seemed amused. "Whew," she said, dropping down in her office chair. "We had an appraiser here all morning, and I've been trying to get all this information typed up." She gave me a rueful smile. "I should have paid more attention in typing class. I didn't know I was going to do that sort of thing for a living." She smiled, but her eyes looked sad. "Models' careers don't last very long."

"You'll get another modeling job," I said quickly. "You are too pretty not to."

"Thanks," she said, really smiling this time. "You know, a different hairdo would do wonders for you." She arranged my hair around my face. "I could fix it for you sometime," she said. "You'd be really pretty if you would just fluff it up a little on the sides. We could try a little makeup, too."

"That would be super," I said. "But I don't think Mom would like the makeup. She thinks I'm too young."

"She must be really old-fashioned." Vicky laughed. "Well, we could do it to see how you look and you could wash it off before you went home."

"Can we do it today?"

"Maybe tomorrow," Vicky said. She waved at the boxes surrounding her desk. "I've got a lot to do today. Miss Murdock is a real slave driver."

"I'd better get to work, anyway," I said, trying to hide my disappointment. "I'm a little late starting."

"She wants you to wipe off the shelves in the hall closet," Vicky said.

"I thought I was supposed to start on the music room."

Vicky shrugged. "Miss Murdock just said the closet. Maybe she wants to tell you what to do in the music room before you start. I think she ought to fill it up with plants; it gets a lot of sun. That used to be the library," she added casually. "Miss Murdock said her grandmother decided the other room was cozier." She went on talking, but my head was spinning with the news. No wonder I hadn't found anything. I'd been looking in the wrong room.

"I guess they didn't have much to do in the old days except read. I don't read much myself," Vicky said.

"I'd better get to work." I tried not to sound too

eager. Vicky shrugged and went back to her desk, and I walked down the hall to check the closet.

Grimy dirt and cobwebs met my eyes when I opened the door. From the looks of it no one had cleaned the closet for fifty years. This was going to be a bigger job than I had thought.

With a sigh I headed to the kitchen for cleaning supplies.

Parts of the house were still gloomy and creepy but there were other parts I loved. Miss Murdock's bedroom and the library were my favorites, followed closely by the kitchen. It had been modernized even before Miss Murdock moved in. "I'm a terrible enough cook on a good stove," Miss Murdock had told me, laughing. So the kitchen boasted modern steel sinks and even a microwave, but it also had a huge stone fireplace with a raised hearth big enough to sit on, and brick floors.

I carried a bucket and scrub brush back down the hall. Vicky's office was empty. Then I saw her through the library window as I walked down the hall, leaning against a tree talking to Mr. Henshaw. They seemed awfully friendly. Suddenly they both laughed. I watched them for a minute and thought about Miss Murdock getting her hair fixed for her date.

I stood there for several minutes before I realized I was passing up a good opportunity to check the music room. I took a rag with me, so I could say I had noticed some dirt if someone came in.

A huge baby grand piano stood in one corner,

still covered with a white cloth. The only other furniture was a few uncomfortable-looking straight-backed chairs pushed over against one corner. The walls in this room were covered with rich dark paneling, with each section set off by wide molding. Now that I was looking in the right place it only took a minute to discover that if I pushed on the third panel, it swung open like a revolving door. I almost fell into the secret room.

EIGHT

Spy Poison

The room was small and narrow, with only a small stream of light from the odd-shaped window to cut through the gloom. It was disappointing, after all our speculation, to find such an unimpressive room. The first Mr. Murdock obviously had not been interested in luxury when he built his get-away. I had been right about one thing, though. It was obviously now some kind of laboratory. The tables inside were covered with neatly arranged bottles and test tubes. There was one other thing that struck me as curious. The opposite wall was decorated in a kind of white tile, like a bathroom. But there were pictures on some of the tiles. I still had not stepped into the room, but the light from the octagonal window shone directly on them, making it easy to see. There were trains, and some of the tiles had pictures of railway stations with the names underneath. I could see the one for Lexing-

ton right in the middle. Then I remembered. The first Mr. Murdock had built his fortune on trains.

I heard the click and heavy creak of the front door. Heart pounding, I swung the panel closed and hurried back out into the hall. I was wringing out my rag when Miss Murdock came around the corner, her arms full of packages.

"Been shopping," she said gaily.

"Looks like you bought the whole store," I said.

Miss Murdock blushed. "Just a couple of new dresses."

I thought of Mr. Henshaw laughing with Vicky and didn't answer. Then I shook myself. Here I was wasting pity on a drug dealer. It was pretty clear that our suspicions had been right.

Danny was still bundled up in bed, looking miserable, when I got home. He put down the puzzle book he'd been working on and stared at me when I told him my news. It didn't cheer him up a bit. "You should have waited for me," he wailed. "I was the one that figured out about the hidden room."

"I didn't go in," I said. "Maybe we can check it out tomorrow if you're better."

"It's not the same."

"I'm sorry. It was just that I had such a good chance to look," I explained. "Vicky was outside and Miss Murdock was gone."

"Tell me again about the wall."

I sighed. "It was just pictures of railway stations. Each one had a name of a nearby town. There was one for Lexington, for Pleasant Valley, for Simpson. Everywhere his trains stopped, I suppose."

"Did you see anything else? I mean like a trap-door or something?"

I shook my head. "I wasn't in there long enough. But what makes you think there would be a trap-door?"

"There must be another way out of the room," Danny said. His voice was thoughtful. "Remember Mrs. Endslow's story about old Mr. Murdock disappearing?"

"I forgot about that," I admitted.

"Maybe the trains on the wall mean something." Danny's brow was furrowed with thought.

"Yeah. It means he liked trains. Or railway stations," I added. "I didn't see anything else. I am more interested in what Miss Murdock is doing in there. Do you think we should tell somebody about the lab?"

"What would we tell? It's not against the law to have a laboratory. We've got to get in there and see what she's doing. If we tell now, no one will believe us and she will know we are suspicious."

Danny assured Mom that his flu was the twenty-four-hour kind, even though he was not feeling as well as he pretended. The next afternoon he went with me to the Murdock house. I'd called Jason the night before and told him about my discovery. When we arrived at the house he hurried over to greet us. "Be careful," he warned quietly.

"We will," I promised. Mr. Bemiss was clearing

brush not too far from where we had found the well. I wondered if he had seen it yet. It seemed better to leave it hidden. The well was such a delightful surprise hidden in the weeds and brush. It was like stumbling on a pot of gold on your front porch, all the nicer because it wasn't expected.

Miss Murdock let us in. "I'm lining the shelves in the kitchen," she said. "I sent Vicky to buy some groceries, so I want to get done before she gets back. Would you mind dusting the chairs and piano in the music room?"

Hardly able to believe our good luck, we hurried to the room, and a second later we were in the laboratory.

"Wow," Danny exclaimed. "What do you suppose all this is for?"

"I don't know," I said, sniffing the contents of some beakers.

"I'll bet it's poison," Danny joked half seriously. "Maybe she really makes poison for spies. They keep it in a hollow tooth in case they get caught."

"Quit kidding around," I said as I walked around looking in some beakers. "Listen for Miss Murdock."

But Danny followed me around the room until I stopped by a bowl that contained some gooey red stuff. "I wonder what this is?" I said, bending down for a closer look.

"It doesn't look like any drugs I ever heard about," Danny said.

"Actually, I think this is lipstick."

93

"Lipstick?"

I touched the red glob with my fingertips. "I'm sure of it."

"Maybe it's poison lipstick. They give it to some lady and when she licks her lips . . . ugggg." He held his throat and pretended he was strangling.

I could not help giggling at his antics. But my laugh turned into my own imitation of someone strangling a second later.

"It's not poison," said Miss Murdock from the opening in the wall. "Or drugs. It is just plain, ordinary lipstick."

I almost jumped out of my skin, but Danny stayed amazingly cool.

"Lipstick? That's all?" He sighed. "We thought you were doing something awful."

"Danny!" I cried. "I'm sorry, Miss Murdock. I guess you think we're awful."

Miss Murdock regarded us thoughtfully. "I suppose it did look very sinister. I forgot how curious children can be."

It was difficult to tell if she was angry. I tried not to look too disappointed. Lipstick is not the sort of thing that makes a good mystery.

"We thought you were making drugs," Danny blurted out.

Miss Murdock chuckled. "Then this must be something of an anticlimax. But lipstick is no small matter. Women all over the world have a problem. They put on their lipstick to look nice, and what happens? It disappears in a few hours. But I am working on a revolutionary new formula. It will be worth millions of dollars when it's done. That's why, when my father and I suspected a rival company had learned of our research, we were afraid they might steal the formula. Grandfather had died and bequeathed me this house. No one knew me here, and I really did want to fix up the house and sell it. It seemed like the perfect solution. Besides my father, only Vicky knows what I am doing. And now you, of course. I hope you will give me your word not to say anything."

"We promise," I said. Then I remembered Jason. "Can we tell just Jason? He knows about the laboratory."

"All right," Miss Murdock agreed. "But no one else. I doubt that my competitors would have tracked me all the way to Lexington. It's a safe enough place, but I would still feel safer if no one else knew. In a few more days it won't matter, anyway. The formula has been completed and I'm just testing it now."

"Then you are not angry with us?" I asked.

"No, of course not," she said. "You remind me of myself at your age. I would have been intrigued by a good mystery, too."

"What about the ghost lights?" I asked. "People have been seeing them since your grandfather died. And I saw them the other night when you weren't home."

Miss Murdock frowned. "I've heard of those lights. Do you mean to say you have actually seen them?"

When we nodded she looked thoughtful. "I have to admit this house is strange. A couple of times I thought I could hear people walking. The footsteps seemed to come from everywhere. Scared me, a little. I searched the entire house, including the hidden room, but I didn't find anything. But I am sure there is some logical explanation. Probably just that the house is so old."

"My grandma's house is old. It creaks and snaps and sometimes it even groans. But it never has moving lights or footsteps echoing around," Danny said. He was staring at the wall with the railroad design. "This is neat."

"I was always forbidden to touch it when I was young. I think it broke Grandfather's heart when the railroads began to decline in this country. He inherited two great passions from my great-grandfather, but both of them seem to belong to another time: trains and good manners. He used to tell me that 'please' and 'thank you' were the magic words."

The doorbell rang and Miss Murdock hurried off to answer it, first shooing us back into the music room and sliding the panel back in place. "I know I can trust you to keep my secret," she said as she left.

Danny pulled a stubby pencil and a tiny notebook out of his pocket and started scribbling.

"What are you doing?" I asked.

"Do you remember any of the names on the wall? I want to write them down before I forget."

"Haven't we acted foolishly enough already?"

"Come on, Cassie. It's important," Danny insisted.

I shrugged. "I think there was Emerald Creek and Opal. And Lexington, of course. Those are the only ones I can remember."

Danny scribbled again. When we heard Miss Murdock returning he quickly stuffed the notebook into his back pocket.

Miss Murdock was smiling. Mr. Henshaw was with her and instead of his usual work clothes he was wearing a suit.

"This is Cassie, the girl who has been such a help," she told him. "And this is her brother, Danny."

"I'm surprised you found such good helpers," Mr. Henshaw said. "Most kids think this house is haunted."

"We don't believe in ghosts," I said primly.

Mr. Henshaw chuckled. "A hard worker and brave, too." He said it like a compliment, but it didn't feel like one. I decided I didn't like Mr. Henshaw very much. He was handsome in a rough sort of way, but he didn't seem the sort to like quiet, plain Miss Murdock. Maybe he liked her because she was rich. I shrugged. Miss Murdock seemed to like him. It wasn't any of my business, anyway. I'd done enough snooping for one day.

"Why don't you sit in the living room," Miss Murdock told him. "I want to talk to the children a minute."

"I just remembered something," I said when he had gone. "Are you sure no one else knows what you are doing?" I told her about the conversation we had overheard in the woods.

"That does sound odd," Miss Murdock said thoughtfully. "But I checked Mr. Bemiss's references very carefully. He is an awful grump, I know, but he's doing a marvelous job on the grounds."

"We could watch him for you," Danny said.

"No, we won't," I said quickly. "We have had enough mysteries. We will just do our work, and go home."

Miss Murdock smiled and patted my shoulder. "Maybe I should mention it to Mr. Henshaw, and ask him to keep an eye on him. Now," she said briskly. "I found another box of books that need to be shelved. I put them in the library. Some of them are very old, so handle them carefully."

Miss Murdock hurried back to the living room. I could hear her talking to Mr. Henshaw as we went next door to the library.

"Hey, Cassie," Danny yelled a few minutes later. He was sitting on the library floor looking at one of the books. "It's a book of manners. Listen to this:

"I think it would be lots of fun
To be polite to everyone;
A boy would doff his little hat,

A girl would curtsy just like that.
And both would use words such as these;
'Excuse me sir,' and 'If you please,'
Not only just at home you know,
But everywhere that they should go."

"I guess most people were pretty fussy about manners in old Mr. Murdock's day," I said. "If we lived back then you would have had to help me into my chair and kiss my hand."

"Forget that," Danny said with a snort. "You can kiss your own hand."

NINE

Mr. Murdock's Secret

Mr. Henshaw's partner, Dave, was piling tools into the pickup as we left. I looked up at the roof. It didn't seem like they'd made much progress. If Mr. Henshaw kept on dating Miss Murdock it was going to take them a year to finish the roof.

Jason was just as disappointed as we were to learn the real purpose of the secret room. "So much for that mystery." He sighed.

"Maybe not," Danny said. "We still haven't figured out how old Mr. Murdock got out of the room. Remember Miss Murdock said she wasn't allowed to touch the railway wall? I've been thinking about it. I'll bet there is an opening in that wall."

I shook my head. "On the other side of the wall is the living room. That's the last place Mr. Murdock would have wanted to go."

Danny was quiet for a minute. "Then maybe it's

some kind of code telling how to get out of the room."

"Where would he go if he did get out?" asked Jason.

Danny shrugged. "Maybe to another secret room."

"Here we go again," Jason said with a groan.

"Forget it, Danny," I said. "It's a wonder she didn't fire me as it is. A few more days and I will have all the money I need."

"Why do you need the money?" Jason asked. "You never did tell me."

I hesitated. I knew he worked to help out his mother. Charm school didn't seem very important next to that. But before I could think of an answer, Danny told him.

"Shut up, Danny," I squealed. Then, trying to regain some dignity, I said, "They teach you other things besides charm."

Jason looked at me out of the corner of his eye. "It isn't going to make you stuck-up, is it?"

"Of course not. It's going to give me poise and confidence. I'll still be me."

"That's the reason I like you," Jason said. "A lot of girls are stuck-up, but you are just a . . . regular person," he finished, his face a little red. "Anyway, if charm school isn't going to change you, why go?"

I tried to explain why it was so important, but I could see that in spite of Jason's polite, understanding nods he did not understand. After we said good-bye, I thought about it some more. Actually, I was hoping Mrs. DuPrey's school would change me. But I would never change so much I didn't like Jason. It was strange to think about it. A few weeks ago Sara and I had been best friends. Now my best friends were a boy and my very own brother. And maybe one other. Missy Ryan had been sitting with me every day at lunch. We'd found out that we liked a lot of the same things. I was sorry I couldn't tell her about Miss Murdock.

I didn't pay much attention to Danny's idea of another hidden room. I figured he'd forget it since our last attempt at playing detective had turned out to be a dud. Things went pretty much back to normal until Friday evening.

After dinner I saw him with a pile of newspapers on his lap. He had an excited expression I was beginning to recognize.

"Look at this," he demanded, shoving today's paper under my nose.

" 'Art Gallery robbed just before dawn,' " I read out loud. " 'Police suspect same burglars who have been victimizing wealthy residents for the past few months.' So? What has that got to do with us?"

Danny's eyes were positively sparkling. "Ever since Dawn's uncle was robbed something about these burglaries has been bothering me, but I couldn't figure out what. So I went through the stack of newspapers Mom has for recycling and found this. Here, read it yourself."

I quickly scanned the crumpled paper, slightly

102

yellowed with age. It was dated a couple of months before, when the robberies first started. A jewelry store had been broken into. The private security guard from the building next door had seen the burglars and had chased them, but he had lost them near Elm and Fifth.

"That's right by the Murdock house," I said.

"Exactly," Danny said. "That's what made me remember it."

"You think the burglars are hiding the loot at the Murdock house?"

"Yes, and they made the ghost lights to scare people away," Danny said. "Remember, the lights started after Mr. Murdock died. And that was also about when the burglaries started."

It did make a weird kind of sense. "But the light was in the secret room," I said. "And we saw in there. Remember? No loot, just lipstick. And who would be doing it, anyway?" Then I knew the answer. "Mr. Bemiss," I exclaimed.

"That must be what the conversation was about." Danny snapped his fingers. "Bemiss and his friend wanted to do this robbery, but they were afraid Miss Murdock was getting suspicious."

Suddenly my face fell. "It still doesn't work. Miss Murdock would surely know if a bunch of crooks were loading stuff into her house."

"What if they didn't have to go in through a door? What if there is some other way to the secret room from the outside?"

"There isn't. Jason checked the outside wall. It

103

is all brick and stone. You would be able to see a crack if there was an opening. But he checked carefully and there isn't."

"I know I'm right," Danny said stubbornly. "I wish we could watch the house tonight. Maybe they didn't have time to hide the stuff before daylight."

"Are you crazy? Do you know how cold it is out there? Besides, it's going to snow, and you just got over the flu."

"All right. Then I'll go see if I can figure out the code," he said. I stared after him as he went to his room. He had agreed to give up too easily. One thing I had recently learned about my brother was that when he gets an idea he holds on to it like a dog holds on to his bone. Then I shrugged. His weird idea about the railway wall containing some sort of code would keep him busy for a while.

"Cassie, wake up," Danny whispered in my ear. I cracked open one eye. It seemed like I had barely drifted off to sleep. Danny's coat and hair were soaked with melting snowflakes as he stood over my bed. I jumped up, awake instantly. "You are dripping on me. Why are you all wet?" I demanded. I was still groggy with sleep. I squinted at the clock. "No wonder I'm so sleepy. Do you realize what time it is? It's not even five o'clock." Then the meaning of the dripping coat dawned on me. "You've already been out," I whispered. "Mom and Dad will kill you if they find out."

"I had to go, Cassie. I kept thinking about the burglaries and I knew I was right."

"Well, were you?"

Danny grinned, obviously enjoying prolonging the suspense. "I was hiding in the woods on the other side of the house, near where Bemiss met that man. There was a good moon so I could see the house plainly. It was freezing and I just about gave up and went home. And then a car pulled up along the road with its lights off. Two men got out and started carrying things, not to the house like I expected, but into the woods."

"Into the woods?"

"Yeah. I couldn't see exactly where. It was too dark and I wasn't about to move."

"Could you see what kinds of things they were carrying?"

"Not too well. But there were some boxes and some big pictures."

"The art gallery," I breathed. "Danny, you are a genius. Was it Mr. Bemiss?"

"I couldn't tell. It was too dark and they both had scarves around their faces to keep warm. They had to make a couple of trips to carry everything."

I grabbed my robe and we tiptoed to the kitchen. "I'll make us some breakfast," I said quietly. "You'd better sit by the heater until you quit shivering. Then maybe we ought to wake up Mom and Dad and have them call the police."

"Not yet," Danny said. "They might not believe us without proof. And I'd be in trouble for sneaking out. I don't know exactly where they took the stuff. As soon as it's light we can follow their tracks in the snow. They can't say much if we find the stuff on an early-morning walk. Why don't you call Jason and see if he can meet us there? I'll bet there is a reward for that stuff. He needs it worse than we do."

I looked at him and smiled. "How come I never noticed what a nice kid you are?"

Danny made a wicked face to hide his embarrassment. "Because I'm not usually."

We waited impatiently for the first rays of morning light. I rehearsed my speech for Jason's mother, about an early-morning skating practice while there was no one around to embarrass Jason by watching. But after four rings Jason's sleepy voice croaked hello. When I explained the reason for the call, however, he sounded wide awake. "Did I wake up your mother?"

"I don't think so. She was up late studying," he said. "I'll meet you in ten minutes."

I jumped into my clothes and bundled myself against the cold. Danny and I ran to the corner but Jason was already waiting. "What took you so long?" he teased.

I had on my new parka. It was to have been a birthday present but Mom and Dad had given it to me early. It was thick and warm but even so I was shivering. Jason had only his threadbare old coat and I knew he must be really cold. The sun was just breaking over the horizon but it wasn't going to do much good today. There was nearly four inches of new snow on the ground.

"Let's hurry. We'll find where they hid the stuff and go back to my house and call the police," I said. My teeth were chattering with the cold and with fear.

"And have some hot cocoa," Danny said, as we reached the Murdock property.

"Sounds great." Jason bent down to study the tracks. They led straight into Miss Murdock's woods. "I want to make sure they didn't return after Danny went home to get you." After a minute he straightened up. "The tracks are partly covered with snow, so they must have dumped the loot and left." He pointed to the tracks. "This man had a half-moon shape on the bottom of his shoe. See, you can count the trips he made. There are the two sets going into the woods, and two coming back."

"That's pretty good," I said.

"My dad used to teach me stuff like that." He stood up. "Let's go, before we freeze to death. We'll find the stuff and get right back home and call the police."

"We'd still better be careful in case they come back," I said.

We sloughed through the snow, keeping the tracks in sight. I figured they were leading to the toolshed or to the deep thickets just beyond, but to my amazement the tracks turned toward the house.

"They are heading for the well," Jason said, stopping suddenly.

"What well?" Danny asked.

"I guess we forgot to tell you," I said. "We found this real cute little well one day. But we didn't have a chance to go back and check it out better."

"Why would they go there?"

"There was a ladder inside," Jason said. "Remember?"

"You should have told me about the well," Danny grumbled. He sounded excited. "That's just what I was looking for."

"What do you mean?" asked Jason.

"A way into the house."

"It's way over at the edge of the woods," I said. "How is that going to get them into the house?"

Jason snapped his fingers. "A tunnel. It makes sense. I figured they just dumped the stuff inside the well. But maybe it does lead to the house somehow."

Excited, we hurried on. I glanced at the house, nervously wondering if we could be seen now that some of the brush had been cleared. But the house was dark and silent. With luck Vicky and Miss Murdock were still asleep.

When we got to the well, we peered over the edge, uncertain what to do. "I wish we had a flashlight," I said.

Danny fumbled in his pockets and presented one with a flourish. "I had it last night. Lucky I forgot to put it away when I came home."

"The ladder goes all the way to the bottom," Jason said. "But I don't see anything down there." He played the light around the walls.

"Do you think we should climb down and take a look?" I asked, hoping Jason would say no. But he nodded and lowered himself over the side. As I swung over the edge and felt for the first step, I couldn't help wishing I would wake up and find myself safe in bed. The light dimmed as I descended and there was a faint musty smell as I neared the bottom. I clung to the decrepit boards, listening to them creak and groan with our weight.

"I don't think I can make it," I moaned.

"Just a few more steps," Jason's comforting voice said from below. "I'm on the bottom." He held the ladder while I lowered myself the last few steps.

"Now what?" asked Danny, jumping down beside me. There was barely enough room for the three of us to move around. I ran my hands over the stone walls. "It's just a dead end," I said, my excitement sagging. "There is nothing here but an old dry well."

TEN

The Tunnel

"I was so sure we'd find the loot here," Jason said, sounding equally disappointed.

"There has to be some kind of opening," Danny said. "Why else would the footsteps lead here?"

"Wait," Jason said. "There is some sort of handle here, by my foot." He bent over and tugged.

"Try pushing down," I suggested when nothing happened. Jason stepped down hard. Immediately there was a scraping noise like stones rubbing together. Heart pounding, I watched a narrow doorway slowly slide open.

"I was right," Danny whispered triumphantly, peering into the blackness. "There is a tunnel." He flashed his light around the entrance, revealing an electric lantern in a niche above the opening.

Jason reached up and switched it on and the tunnel was flooded with light. "This proves someone's been down here lately. The battery is still good."

"Maybe we should just go back and get some help," I said.

Jason didn't seem to have heard me. He took a few tentative steps into the tunnel, then walked faster. I followed, stumbling sometimes in my efforts to keep up. Danny trailed behind me. Ahead, the light from Jason's lantern cast an eerie glow, and long shadows played along the dark walls.

"I don't like this," I said. "I keep hoping this is all a dream."

Jason's chuckle floated back. "Feel your fingers. If they are as numb as mine, that ought to convince you we're awake."

"Maybe we are all crazy," Danny offered.

"For once we agree," I told him. I was so busy shivering that when Jason suddenly stopped I almost crashed into him.

"Look at this," he shouted. He held the light over his head to illuminate several steps leading into inky darkness. We waited while he climbed them.

"There is some kind of catch above my head," he called.

Then I heard a scraping sound and a minute later Jason's voice, sounding hollow and far away.

"It's the music room. There is a trapdoor in the floor. But it is cut so cleverly that it looks like the seams in the wood floors," he said as he backed down the stairs. "Bemiss must have found the trapdoor when he was hiding things in the tunnel. Somehow he knew about the hidden room. Maybe he just slipped up to snoop around now and then."

"And people saw the light and thought the house was haunted," I exclaimed. "But we still haven't found whatever he hid down here."

"The tunnel goes on." Danny spoke for the first time in a while. "It must go under the secret room."

Something soft and furry brushed against my leg. I couldn't stop myself from screaming, but Danny grabbed my hand. "It's only the cat, look," he said. He flashed his light and I saw two glowing green eyes. Still shaking, I bent down and stroked his head. "That solves that mystery," I said. My voice was still shaking. I told them about Lucifer's sudden appearance in the library.

Danny walked back a few feet and flashed his light overhead. "I can see a short pipe. Must be left over from some old ventilation system. But it's got rusty holes big enough for a cat to squeeze through. This wall is so rough he could have climbed back up. I'll bet he was hunting rats," he said wickedly, grinning at me.

Rats didn't bother me half as much as the thought of Bemiss coming back. But Danny glanced nervously around as though he had frightened himself.

"I hope nobody heard me scream," I said.

Jason chuckled. "I doubt it. But if they did they would think you were a ghost."

Danny was shining his light on the top of the tunnel. "Those boards look pretty rotten. Let's hurry up. This place gives me the creeps."

We had only taken a few more steps when we

stumbled into a small room with a dirt floor. I heard a squeak and something furry scurried out of the light. Danny had guessed the reason for Lucifer's attraction to the air vent.

"See if that stuff is what we are looking for," I said. There were several boxes lined up against the wall and piled in the corner.

"Better not touch anything," Jason warned, too late to stop Danny, who had opened one bag and was holding a handful of old coins.

"I'll bet these are part of the coin collection that was stolen from Dawn's uncle," Danny said. He dropped the coins back into the sack. "But you are right. We don't want to mess up any evidence."

"I'm scared," I admitted. "We'd better get some help right away."

Jason nodded seriously, and a few minutes later we had retraced our steps through the tunnel. Jason carefully replaced the lantern and we climbed the ladder to the top. Jason peeked cautiously over the edge. "Still no one around," he said. He sounded relieved. I was not the only one who was nervous.

"Look, Bemiss doesn't get to work until about eight," Danny said. "Maybe we should just go to the house and ask Miss Murdock to call the police instead of walking all the way home. We know she's not involved. The robberies started before she came to Lexington."

I nodded as I climbed out after him, and we crossed the yard. The truck lettered "Bob and Dave

Construction" was just pulling into the driveway when we reached the walk. Bob Henshaw gave us a startled glance, but we kept on walking to the front door.

I rang the bell and waited. Henshaw and his helper Dave unloaded some ladders, watching us curiously. I had to ring the bell again before a disheveled and sleepy Vicky finally opened the door. She was tying the belt around her robe, and she looked irritated. "What on earth are you kids doing here at this time in the morning?" she said.

"Where's Miss Murdock?" I blurted out. "She should call the police."

A strange look passed over her pretty features. "Miss Murdock is not here. Mr. Bemiss drove her to the airport very early. Her father is arriving for a surprise visit. And what is this about the police?"

Quickly Jason explained. As the story tumbled out Vicky listened carefully, her face expressionless.

"First things first," she said when we were finished. "You all look half frozen. I'll make you a cup of cocoa. Then, while you are drinking that, I'll call the police for you. They may not believe a bunch of kids."

"You believe us, don't you?" I asked.

Vicky bustled about the kitchen heating milk and measuring the cocoa. She didn't answer for so long I was afraid she was going to say no. But finally she set the cups in front of us and nodded. "Of course I believe you. Miss Murdock is going to be surprised when she finds out that her gardener is a crook."

She picked up the phone and started to dial. Then she tapped the disconnect switch several times. "The phone's dead," she said. "Must be the storm."

"Oh, no," I groaned. "What should we do now?"

Vicky snapped her fingers. "I know. Bob Henshaw has a CB in his truck. You finish your cocoa, and I'll go tell him what's going on."

"How does she know Mr. Henshaw has a CB?" Danny asked when she had slipped on a coat and boots and stepped outside.

"I think they like each other," Jason said. "I've seen them talking."

"Yeah," I said glumly. "So have I."

I paced the floor impatiently. It was taking an awfully long time. "If they would hurry, the police would be waiting when Bemiss gets back," I said.

Danny stepped over to the phone and picked up the receiver. "Hey, it's working again," he said, just as Vicky walked back in. Mr. Henshaw and Dave loomed in the doorway behind her.

"Bob thinks he'd better take a look at the stuff before we notify the police," she said. "We could all get in a lot of trouble if the things you found are not really stolen."

"It would be very embarrassing to Miss Murdock if it was a mistake," Mr. Henshaw said.

116

"But we should—" Danny said, but Henshaw interrupted. "It won't hurt to make sure. How did you kids find out, anyway? You must be pretty good little detectives. Won't your parents worry with you out so early?"

"We didn't tell them we were coming here," Jason said honestly. "We didn't really figure it out until this morning. We knew Bemiss was up to something, but we weren't sure what it was."

"Bemiss? He is a rather unpleasant fellow at that. Miss Murdock asked me to keep an eye on him just last night. That's why she had him drive her to the airport. She wanted a chance to find out more about him. You kids will probably get a reward," Mr. Henshaw said.

Reluctantly we put our coats back on and led Mr. Henshaw and his silent helper to the well.

"We are wasting time," I said. "What if Bemiss comes back?"

"We'll just take a quick peek," Henshaw said. He climbed over the edge of the well and started down the ladder. Jason, Danny, and I climbed after him, and Dave came last.

Henshaw reached into the niche where Jason had replaced the lantern and switched it on. I felt a cold chill run down my spine. He had known exactly where it was hanging.

"I've been wondering how Mr. Bemiss found out about the well," I said. "You were the one who played here when you were young. If anyone knew about the well, it should be you." The minute I said it I wished I could bite back the words. Henshaw held the lantern over his head and looked back at us.

"As I said, you are pretty sly little detectives. Too bad no one will ever know."

ELEVEN

Trapped!

Henshaw and Dave herded us back to the room filled with the loot. "What are you going to do with us?" Danny said boldly.

"I've been thinking about that," Bob Henshaw said. "I think there is going to be an unfortunate accident. Maybe a little cave-in. Everyone will search, but eventually they will decide you all just ran away. Who knows, maybe someday they'll find a bunch of bones and decide you were the ghosts of the Murdock house."

"You can't do that," I spluttered.

"She's right," Dave finally said. "Stealing is one thing, but this is too much."

I looked at him gratefully, but Henshaw whirled around to face him and snarled, "You ready to go to jail for twenty years?"

Dave was silent for a second. He didn't look at us. "All right," he said. "But you do it. I don't want any part of it." Then he paused. "What about the woman?"

"She won't say anything. Lovely Lady Cosmetics has offered her fifty thousand for that formula."

"She was pretty squeamish about the kids," Dave said.

Henshaw looked thoughtful. "You're right. Well, we'll just take care of her, too. No reason we can't sell that formula ourselves."

I sagged against the boxes. I had been telling myself that we would be all right because Vicky would rescue us. Beautiful Vicky. I had admired her, looked up to her, and she was nothing but a common crook. I thought of the day I had seen her laughing with Henshaw. Had they decided even then to protect each other's secrets?

"Start loading some of this stuff out," Henshaw told Dave. "We won't be able to get all of it, but take the coins and jewels." He took some rope from a box and while Dave silently carried loot back through the tunnel, Henshaw tied our hands and feet.

"What if we promised not to tell?" I asked desperately.

"Sorry, kid. I couldn't trust you," Henshaw said with a shrug.

"Our parents will be looking for us soon," Danny said. "I left a note."

Mr. Henshaw paused ever so briefly. "I don't think so. I think you were having too much fun playing junior detective."

"What about Miss Murdock? If you know about the tunnel, then so must she."

Henshaw shook his head. "Wrong again. I found it accidentally one day, long after she stopped coming to visit the old man. I never told. The Murdocks always thought they were so smart with all their money. But now we see who was really the smartest."

I bit my lip and fell silent. Jason gave me a weak smile. He had been struggling against his bonds, and when Henshaw left with a load of loot he twisted slightly to show me he was almost free.

"Look at the wall," Danny whispered. I twisted around, but then Dave came back again with Henshaw right behind him.

"It's a shame to leave all the rest of this stuff, but I think we have enough to make us rich for a long, long time," he said.

"How are you going to cave it in?" Dave asked him.

"Those boards up there are pretty old and rotten," Henshaw said. He knocked on the overhead boards and tiny trickles of sand and dust sifted down. "I think if we get these down, the whole tunnel will cave in right here. Then if we do the same at the entrance to the well it ought to be pretty well sealed off."

That was when I finally believed him. None of us even screamed or cried. We just sat in terrified horror as the two men rocked the frame around the room's entrance. I heard a scrape as the rocks shifted, and the two men jumped back.

"Look out," Dave shouted. There was a rumble and the entrance filled with dirt, rocks, and rotten timbers. We choked and coughed as clouds of dust and dirt filled the air. I waited for the room to come crashing in on us, but amazingly the ceiling remained steady. Only a few grains of dirt trickled down. Then, suddenly, the room was deathly quiet. My heart pounded as I tried to make myself believe it had really happened. We were trapped in an underground room, plunged in a darkness deeper than anything I had ever seen. We were going to die, locked in the black prison until we starved to death or ran out of air.

"I'm almost free," Jason said. His voice sounded hollow in the black emptiness.

"What good will that do?" I said dully. "We are trapped and we're going to die."

"We'll dig our way out. Maybe the whole tunnel didn't collapse. If we can dig to the trapdoor under the music room, maybe we can get out."

"That must be ten feet back in the tunnel. We'll never make it."

"Got any better suggestions?" I heard him wiggle out of the last knots.

"I might," Danny said. His voice was amazingly calm. "That's what I've been trying to tell you. Remember the wall in the secret room, the one that has all the town names on it?"

"What about it?" Jason asked. There was a note of hope in his voice.

"The back wall of this room is just like it. You couldn't see it until they got all those boxes out of here."

"So?" I said. "We already know old Mr. Murdock was crazy about trains."

Jason was free and fumbling with my bonds. Danny went on talking, more to himself than to us. "This is just a crude tunnel with a room cut off to one side. Why would anyone go to all the trouble to make one wall with decorated tiles?"

Jason's hands stopped working. "You're right. You think there's a room on the other side?"

"No," Danny said thoughtfully. "I still think the names of the different railway stations are a code."

"A code for what?" I asked, daring to hope at last.

"I think the town names can be arranged to open the wall," Danny said. "I was playing around with them the other night and I noticed something."

"Even if you are right," I said bitterly, "it is so dark in here we can't even see the wall."

"If someone would just untie me they might have a surprise," Danny said. "Like my flashlight is still in my coat pocket."

Jason crawled over to Danny and a minute later a faint light cut through the darkness. "Danny, you are terrific," I said. The light, faint as it was, filled me with hope. "Now if you can get us out of here, I might even give you a kiss."

"Please," Danny joked. "A simple thank-you will do." He took a stubby pencil out of another pocket, and a scrap of paper. "Remember how Miss Murdock said her grandfather had two passions: trains and good manners? And how he was always saying that 'please' and 'thank you' were the magic words? Now a lot of parents say that, even Mom and Dad. But what if Mr. Murdock really meant it?

"Last night, while I was waiting for Mom and Dad to go to sleep so I could sneak out, I looked at all those station names we wrote down Monday. I'd been staring at them all week, but suddenly the answer dawned on me. Look." He scribbled rapidly and held the light over the paper so we could see.

Pleasant Valley
Lexington
Emmet
Austin
Simpson
Emerson
Opal
Prospect
Emerald Creek
Nesbit

"Please open!" I exclaimed, reading the first letter of each town. "Danny, you are a genius."

Danny shook his fading light. "Let's hope I'm right," he said. His voice sounded grim. "This light isn't going to last much longer."

"Let's try pushing the tiles," Jason said. "Read them off in order."

I had to keep reminding myself to breathe as I watched. Carefully Jason pushed the tiles, one by one. After each one we listened, but there was no sound except the dull thudding of our hearts. Then, as he started on the word "open," I thought I heard a rusty squeal. "It's working," I shouted, as the wall slowly slid back. Danny played his light inside, revealing a narrow set of stairs leading up to a wall I knew was in the secret room.

Pushing cobwebs out of the way, we hurried up the stairs. From this side of the wall no code was needed. There was a handle, thick with dust and rust, which yielded after several tugs. We stumbled gratefully into the thin light streaming through the octagonal window.

"Hoo—" I started to yell, but the final "ray" stuck in my throat, and instead of feeling relief, I groaned. The sliding panel to the secret room was wide open. A tear-stained and pale Vicky Presser stood by one of the tables, and snooping through the papers on the corner desk were Bob Henshaw and Dave.

TWELVE

A Frog
and Two Princes

Vicky spoke first. "You are all right!" She sounded almost happy.

"I thought I took care of you once," Henshaw growled. "But don't worry, I will this time." He took a step forward and tried to grab my arm.

The next few minutes were a blur of confusion and cat fur. Just as Henshaw reached for me, Jason kicked with all his strength. I heard the crack as Jason's boot landed squarely on Henshaw's anklebone. He yelped and bumped into one of the tables, where Lucifer was sitting, calmly giving himself his daily bath. If there is one thing that makes Lucifer angry, it is for someone to disturb his daily bath. So he arched his back and hissed.

Henshaw was still yelling, and by now Vicky was, too, as she struggled with Dave. This proved entirely too much for Lucifer. He jumped, with all of his claws extended, right onto Henshaw's back.

Henshaw cursed and tried to grab for Lucifer with his free hand. For a second I just stood with my mouth open in surprise. Through it all Henshaw had not released his grip on me, but now both Jason and I started kicking and hitting as hard as we could. Now that he had only one hand to protect himself, most of our blows were connecting. Out of the corner of my eye I saw Danny race around the other side of the table to help Vicky.

I finally managed to twist my arm free, and with a last hard kick Jason and I yelled at Danny and raced for the opening. But two steps out of the open panel all three of us ran smack into the arms of a uniformed policeman, who looked utterly flabbergasted.

Miss Murdock, who looked even more astonished, was right behind with another officer, and with her was Mr. Bemiss, his normal scowl twisted into open-mouthed amazement. A neatly dressed older man stood behind them. Of the five people he looked the most calm, and I wondered if he was Miss Murdock's father. For a minute everyone just stared. Then everyone burst out talking at the same time.

"What is going on?" asked Miss Murdock. "What are you children doing here?" Then she noticed Bob Henshaw. "Bob," she said, "what are you doing in my laboratory?"

"He's trying to steal your lipstick formula," I gasped. "Vicky wanted to steal it all along. But then Henshaw double-crossed her."

Miss Murdock looked sad. "Is that true, Vicky?"

Vicky hung her head. "It was so much money. You don't know how I hated the thought of being a secretary the rest of my life."

"My father and I worked out an advertising campaign for the twenty-four-hour lipstick. We were going to aim it at the working woman, and we were going to make you the leading model."

"Why didn't you tell me?" Vicky sobbed as the policeman handcuffed her.

"I was waiting until the formula was done. That's why my father is here. We were going to tell you our surprise. As a reward for all your hard work." Miss Murdock looked almost as upset as Vicky.

"But why are you here?" Jason asked one of the policemen.

"Miss Presser called us. Said she didn't want any part of hurting you kids."

One of the policemen turned to Vicky. "I imagine the judge will take that into consideration," he said. "And your evidence against these two might make for a lighter sentence."

A subdued Vicky, Henshaw, and Dave were led to the squad car. Several other policemen arrived. We had to tell our story several times, and of course everyone wanted us to demonstrate how to unlock the door between the tunnel and the secret room.

"Looks like you kids really had a close call," said one of the policemen. "But at least we got all this gang wrapped up. They won't be going anywhere for a good long time."

129

"I think maybe you missed one of them," I whispered, nodding to Mr. Bemiss. "I think he is one of them, too."

"Oh, I doubt that," the policeman chuckled. "Mr. Bemiss is one of our best detectives. He has been watching the house for weeks."

I looked at Mr. Bemiss. For the first time he was actually smiling.

"I'd been watching Henshaw for a long time and I was pretty sure the loot was being hidden on the Murdock estate, but I never could find out where. We had noticed that the ghost light reports always came after a robbery. But I was watching the house," he said ruefully. "I never looked at the well."

"You children could have been hurt or even killed," Miss Murdock said as she joined us. "I hope this ends your detective work."

"I feel so dumb about Vicky Presser," I said. "I thought she was so nice."

"I don't think Vicky was bad. She did try to help you at the end. I guess she was just weak. But if it is any comfort, she fooled me, too. It's like that old saying, you can't judge a book by its cover. I guess we both paid too much attention to the outside. And Henshaw, too. I was flattered when he paid so much attention to me. But I remembered something this morning. I never liked him very much when he was young, either."

"That's why the lettering on the side of the truck looked so new," Danny said. "There never was any

Bob and Dave Construction Company. They just painted it on the truck so Mr. Murdock would hire them. That was so they could check out the tunnel underneath the house."

"And that's why so little of the roof got done," Miss Murdock said. "Now I will have to find some new roofers, and a new gardener, too. It's a shame," she said, looking at Bemiss with a smile. "If you weren't a policeman, you could have been a wonderful gardener."

The whole story was on the six o'clock news, and all three of us became instant celebrities. Even Dawn and Sara suddenly wanted to be my friends. An insurance company had offered a large reward for the return of some of the valuables, and the mayor decided to give it to us in a big ceremony.

"How do I look?" Mom asked for the third time on the day of the ceremony.

"You look nice," Dad assured her. "Stop being so nervous."

"It's not every day I'm on television," Mom said.

"Thank heaven for that," Dad said. "Anyway, everyone will be looking at our gorgeous daughter." I blushed as I gave myself a final check in the mirror. I had a new dress for the occasion and I was pleased with the way it looked. "Not bad for a frog," I told my image. I wondered if Jason would like it.

But at the ceremony I hardly had a chance to talk to him. The mayor gave a stirring speech and put his arms around us as if he were our father. Danny squirmed uncomfortably, and Jason looked miserable in a new suit. Jason's mother stood next to Mom and Dad, beaming proudly. Halfway through the mayor's speech I saw her give Jason a wink. He winked back, like a secret signal of their love. She looked nice, and I had a hunch she was going to be a terrific teacher someday.

The mayor handed each of us an envelope, and when I peeked in mine I nearly fainted. There was a check for two thousand dollars.

"I'll bet your mom and dad are proud of you," Missy said later that afternoon. We were in my room trying to decide what I should do with all that money.

"Ha!" I laughed. "Dad said I was lucky not to be punished for not telling them what we were up to."

"What are you going to do with all that money?"

"Maybe I could buy a car. I could drive it in four years," I said dreamily.

"You could buy a lot of fancy clothes in case you get to go on television again."

"I have a better idea," Mom said as she passed my room and peeked in. "Let's put the money away for college."

I wasn't too thrilled with that idea, but I had the feeling that was exactly what was going to happen to my new fortune.

"All of it?"

Mom nodded. "All of it. I was going to take a little of it to buy something you needed, but Dad said we could give it to you for an early birthday present." She handed me a little gift-wrapped box.

Eagerly I tore off the paper. Inside the box was a small electric razor. I looked up guiltily, but Mom was smiling.

After Missy left I slipped out the door and ran to the Murdock place. To my surprise Jason was working in the yard.

"Your mom must have made you save your money for college, too," I said.

"Yeah," Jason said glumly. Then he brightened. "It's not so bad. My job was only going to last until Mr. Bemiss got the yard in shape. But since Mr. Bemiss isn't here anymore Miss Murdock said I could work a couple of hours every afternoon as long as she stays. And that might be a long time. She's thinking about keeping the house and running the bed and breakfast inn herself. She says she really likes Lexington. I might have enough to go to the movies once in a while." He paused and looked a little embarrassed. "Would you like to go with me sometime?"

"Me?"

"Of course you. Or will you be too busy going to charm school?"

"I haven't decided about that," I said. "I've been thinking about taking gymnastics lessons instead. I like doing stuff like that."

"We should ask Danny to go with us," Jason said. "He's part of the team."

"That's a good idea," I said. "It would be nice if

we could find another mystery to solve," I added.

Jason shook his head and yelled, "No more mysteries," but he was grinning.

I thought about the old fairy tales—the ones where a princess's kiss turned a frog into a prince. A few weeks ago I had thought it would be nice the other way around—if there were a prince for every frog princess.

Although I didn't really feel like a frog anymore, I was kind of surrounded by royalty. Danny was really a prince of a brother, and as I smiled at Jason I could almost imagine a crown on the top of his head.

"Why are you smiling?" Jason asked.

"I was thinking how much I liked your hat."

Jason tugged off the old baseball cap he always wore. "This old hat?" He looked confused.

I smiled mysteriously. "That one, too," I said.